# ONLY HALF
# A
# HOAX

*Also by L. A. Taylor*
Footnote to Murder

# ONLY HALF
# A
# HOAX

## L. A. Taylor

Walker and Company   New York

3-84 Baker 7.45

First published in the United States of America
in 1983 by the Walker Publishing Company, Inc.

Published simultaneously in Canada by John Wiley & Sons Canada,
Limited, Rexdale, Ontario.

Library of Congress Catalog Card Number: 83-60031

Library of Congress Cataloging in Publication Data
Taylor, Laurie
Only half a hoax
I. Title.
PS3570.A94305 1983      813'.54      83-60031
ISBN 0-8027-5499-6
Printed in the United States of America
10  9  8  7  6  5  4  3  2  1

The places in this novel, except in some details, are real. All
the characters and every one of their actions are entirely fic-
tional and are not based on any real persons or incidents.

# First

IT began, as so many disasters begin, with a coincidence. Two coincidences, really.

The first was that an oriole had arrived early in the spring, far ahead of the rest of its species, and flew from the gutter where it had been drinking into the light green mist of the elm branches, just as one particular car drew up to the stop sign at Grimes and 44th. The second was that this happened at the exact moment it did, a little past one o'clock on a sunny April afternoon.

Anyone would have lifted his eyes to follow that bright orange flash. But what arrested the driver's attention was not the further antics of the bird, but the huge object flying in seeming silence out of the east. Five times the size of a full moon, it looked like nothing more than two enormous Corelle ware saucers cemented together lip to lip, skimming across the sky with the seam tilted slightly forward and with a half sphere of something reflective and silvery on the top. In other words, a classic UFO.

The car radio dissolved into static, under which WCCO faintly continued to give the stockyard report: prices of steers in St. Paul. Barrows and gilts.

The driver had never been a panicker. As the object sailed majestically behind the elm, the car remained where it was and didn't stall. Gleams of white traced the path of the object as it curved behind the elm where the oriole sang, and when it emerged on the other side of the tree, the driver of the little car gasped.

The "flying saucer" was nothing more or less than a Northwest Airlines jumbo jet, complete with the tall red tail that distinguishes that airline's planes from all others even at a distance of several miles. Now the sound could be heard too, a deep roar that drowned 'CCO as the static faded.

The driver sat perfectly still, considering such topics as peculiar reflections of sunlight and incipient insanity, until a station wagon pulled up behind and honked. Then the little car

R297752

moved slowly toward France Avenue, as the driver suddenly realized that coincidence had just presented what promised to be an extremely useful gift, exactly when such a gift was most needed.

To make use of it would take quite a bit of planning. But planning was one thing this driver did very well, and the glimmer of a possible plan had already appeared. The woman at the wheel of the station wagon honked and revved in vain: the two cars continued down 44th at something less than twenty miles an hour as the plan brightened.

The light at France turned green just as the cars approached the intersection. It seemed, almost, an omen.

# I

I peered through one of the tiny, wavery-glass panes at the fat drops kicking up dust in the restaurant parking lot and thanked my stars that I'd brought the umbrella in from the car. A guy in a blue suit dashed across the lot and flung himself through the door beside me just as the deluge descended. Lucky man. "Let's wait until it lets up a little," I said.

Karen, my wife, was watching the guy. She wants to be a writer: she watches people just in case she ever gets around to writing anything, even though she can't spell.

"What's a guy like you doing in a dump like this?" the cashier asked the newcomer.

Dump! I looked around. So, it wasn't Charlie's Café Exceptionale. Just one of a chain of seafood places. But the food was decent, and the atmosphere, though heavy on the bare oak and ferns, wasn't bad. Maybe not *la crème de la crème*, but not cheap, either. Hadn't I just brought my wife, and she what you call heavy with child, into this very restaurant to celebrate our sixth wedding anniversary?

Said wife giggled lightly at something in the cashier's conversation. A gleam of sunlight came through the ersatz-European window. "Let's go," I said to Karen. We left the guy and the cashier getting quietly ribald about the dainty waiter who had served us as much shrimp as we could eat, and pushed out into the damp parking lot.

Karen plopped into the passenger seat and hauled her legs into the car. Usually, she's considerably more graceful, but Joseph Jamison, Jr., was due to be a Yankee Doodle Dandy baby in another couple of weeks, and Karen was a bit of a klutz at the time. I let myself in the driver's side and patted her tummy.

"Not long now."

"Not long." Karen giggled. "What a guy!"

"Me?"

"No, the guy in the restaurant." Well, you can't have everything. "That poor cashier was about melting into the floor; did you notice?"

"No, and I can't see why." I stuck the key into the ignition with a half prayer that the car would start. It doesn't like to get wet.

"Oh, come on, Joe. That guy had to be one of the ten sexiest men on earth." Karen sucked in her cheeks to keep from grinning.

"Don't you melt," I said.

"Don't worry." Karen patted my thigh. "He's the kind that *knows* he's God's gift to women. Too conceited for me. That kind always is."

"Always?" The engine caught, coughed, smoothed out. I smiled at it. Good car.

"Well..." Karen paused. I'm always—and I mean always—teasing her about her tendency to make blanket statements without any evidence. It's the kind of thing I fight against in my hobby, which is investigating UFO sightings. "Often," she amended. "But he had the look. Roses-shall-be-cast-at-my-feet kind of thing."

"I didn't realize you were such a psychologist," I teased. As I backed out of the parking space, the rearview mirror turned a dazzling pink. I snapped it back to get the glare out of my eyes and pulled to the side of the lot. "Now, *there's* something worth looking at," I said, pointing west.

We sat watching the sunset until it faded behind another band of thunderheads heaving over the horizon. Karen glanced at her watch. "We can still catch that spy movie that's showing in Hopkins," she said.

"Sure thing, babe." I made a wide circle through the parking lot and onto the frontage road, where I waited for a break in traffic before sliding onto the highway.

I'm a computer engineer, not a very dedicated one, for one of the big companies here in Minneapolis. Just then the project I was working on was going pretty well: no Saturday overtime. But even though it was Friday and I could take my time persuading the car to start the next morning, I ran the old lemon into the garage to keep it dry and levered myself out between it and the junk that overflows what's supposed to be space for a second car. I'd cleaned the place out just last summer, too. *So, what's an engineer without junk?* I asked myself, tripping over a bale of hay that never got used to mulch the strawberries.

"Here he is," Karen said into the phone as I walked into the kitchen, shaking the rain off the umbrella. She handed me the receiver. "It's for CATCH."

The Committee for Analysis of Tropospheric and Celestial Happenings: CATCH, an optimistic acronym for a bunch of desultory UFO chasers for whom I pretend to be Chief of Field Investigation for Minnesota and the Dakotas, a position that brings me a lot of guff and a few laughs. My hello was on the wary side.

"J. J., it's Mack Forrester," said a resonant baritone. "I got a goodie for you."

I patted my shirt pocket, but the little plastic pouch that holds my pen and ID badge was on the dresser in the bedroom. "Hang on while I find a pencil, will you, Mack?" I said. "Damn house eats pencils."

"Borrow one when you get here," Mack said. "I'm on duty. Just move your ass on out. Busy night."

"Okay. See you."

I walked into the family room. Karen had flipped on the TV; color weather radar made a rainbow blot around the Twin Cities metro area, the kind of thing that throws the local forecasters into ecstasy. "Why can't they just say 'thunderstorms' instead of 'thunderstorm activity'?" Karen asked.

"Search me." Words don't bother me the way they do Karen. I spotted a pencil on top of the TV and pocketed it. "Look, honey," I said, "I'm sorry—I've got to go check out this report."

She groaned. "I hope it didn't land on Mount Rushmore."

"You're in luck," I assured her. "That was Mack, you know. I'm only going as far as St. Louis Park." The TV flashed back to the regularly scheduled program, already in progress.

"A UFO in St. Louis Park, in this weather? You sure you and Mack aren't just going out for a drink?"

"Since when do I go out drinking with Mack?" I asked. "Or anybody else, for that matter? This shouldn't take long." I leaned over the back of the couch. Karen lifted her face, and I brushed a kiss across her mouth. "I won't let it take long."

[9]

"Good."

On the television screen, a black guy with a naked triangular torso seemed to be slathering whipped cream on a dead chicken. I picked my car keys off the kitchen counter and went back out to the garage. *Soon,* I promised myself as I heaved the door up, *I'll get one of those garage-door openers Karen seems to think she's going to need.*

I live on the west side of Minneapolis, not far from Lake Harriet and several blocks south of Lake Calhoun. To the Municipal Building in St. Louis Park is a drive of ten minutes when the lights are with me, and they were with me that night. I parked in one of the spots marked for visitors and found my way in.

Mack Forrester was at the desk, filling out a form. "Those two are yours," he said, pointing to a pair of high school kids, a boy and a girl, standing against one of the dull cream walls.

"Thanks."

Shaking his head, Mack went back to the form. He's an old friend. We grew up next door to each other, only Mack did half a foot more growing than I did and ended up a cop. So though we were best buddies once, we don't see all that much of each other any more. Cops tend to stick to cops, and who can blame them? But Mack promised me a long time ago that he'd let me know the minute any UFO report came in, and this was the third time he'd made good on that promise.

As I crossed the room, the dispatcher's radio crackled: something about an accident. Mack answered in a crisp, detached voice. Robot talk, Karen calls it. I wanted to go home and see what else the guy was going to do to the chicken.

Instead, I said "Hi" to the kids, dug one of my CATCH business cards out of my wallet, and handed it to the boy. "I'm Joseph Jamison, like it says there, and my job is to investigate UFOs. Want to tell me about this one?"

"It was big," the boy said, his eyes as big as saucers, what else? "And it was on the ground."

"A landing?" I said, beginning to get interested. Usually, in St. Louis Park, it's either Venus or landing lights on a plane making an approach to Twin Cities International Airport.

The girl, a petite kid with curly red hair, gave the boy a jab in the ribs. "Tell him where, Ken."

"Oh. Over to Methodist."

"The hospital?"

The boy nodded nervously and took a quick tuck in the corners of his mouth that might have been meant for a smile.

"What were you doing over there?"

"Unh," said the boy, fingering a pimple.

"Visiting somebody?"

"That's right," the girl put in. "But that has nothing to do with this."

*Making out on the edge of the parking lot,* I thought. "And where was the UFO?"

"Unh, kind of in a field."

"It's gone now," the girl said.

I took their names and addresses, in case they changed their minds about wanting to make a full report. "Got time to go back over there and show me exactly where it was?"

They exchanged glances. "Sure," the girl, name of Jodie, decided for them.

"Unh, okay."

I glanced back at Mack as they trailed out the door. He was laughing. Yeah, at me.

I followed their old Ford with my not-so-old Ford, down Highway 100, past 36th Street, where we slowed down for an accident and a lot of flashing lights, and out Excelsior to the hospital. They stopped, as I expected, not far into the lot, which is on the order of a quarter mile deep and nearly as wide.

The rain had slacked off temporarily, and a mist rose over the swaying reeds that border the creek to the west of the parking lot. A humid smell of earth and slow water pervaded the air.

"Came along there," the girl said. She made a wide sweep that took in most of the sea of reeds. I got the idea that the saucer had traveled in a generally southeasterly direction. "It was kind of drifting, like, just above the ground."

"Big," the boy said.

"Not really," Jodie said.

"Then what happened?" I asked, writing all this down in the blue light of the parking lot. A mosquito tried to bite my notepad, and I squashed it into a smear of purple blood.

"It went out."

"It took off."

Simultaneous statements. I turned to the boy. "You saw it take off?"

"Yeah, it went straight up."

"No, it just went out," the girl insisted.

"You blinked."

"I did not."

I walked to the edge of the lot and looked out over the reeds. In daylight, the redwing blackbirds that nest in the cattails can be a real hazard, diving out of the blue to peck at people who venture too close to their territory. This was one of your darker nights, and the birds had presumably slept through the visitation. Though how any living creature could sleep through the racket of insects in that swamp is beyond me. I wondered what an insomniac blackbird might have thought of the saucer.

"How do you know it was a UFO?" I asked, walking back to the kids.

"It was the right shape, like you see in the papers, you know?" Jodie reported with considerable verve. "And all orange and glowing. And you could see lights going around the top of it, sort of, and blinking. White and green lights, just like you read about."

*Pretty elaborate doings,* I thought. I asked them the rest of my questions and gave them each a form to fill out and a stamped envelope to mail it back in, and bid them goodbye. They drove off to find some less exciting place to park, and I got back in my car, which started, and drove slowly toward the hospital building. Not far from where I'd parked, I passed a glistening Toyota Celica with Illinois plates. What kind of good thing could put an out-of-state car in a hospital parking lot? None I could think of. Poor bugger.

As I pushed through the glass entrance doors I thought of a good reason: *come to see a grandchild. At this hour of the night, Jamison?* You've got babies on the brain. I headed automatically for the information desk.

[ 12 ]

Nobody there, of course. It was getting on toward midnight. As I hesitated, a nurse squeaked across the lobby in rubber-soled shoes and glanced at me. "Can I help you?" she asked.

I dug one of the CATCH cards out of my wallet and handed it to her. She read it and frowned.

"Somebody reported a UFO landing next to the hospital earlier this evening," I explained. "A little before eleven. You wouldn't have heard anything about it, would you?"

She grinned. "I didn't come up for air from eight until just now. Emergency's a zoo. High school graduations. But I didn't see any little green men with blood-pressure cuffs on, if that helps."

I gestured west. "It was on that side, anyway."

"Over there, either they sank in the muck or they fell in the creek and drowned," she said. "What about people in those apartment houses?"

"I'll get to them."

"Hold on," she offered. "Maybe I can find you something. Maternity faces that way, and they can go to bed when they please."

I hung around, gathering the suspicion of a security guard, while the nurse disappeared for a few minutes. The gift shop was closed. The snack bar was closed. They hadn't covered up the laudatory brass plaques, though, so I read all about the founding and accomplishments of the hospital and staff. I was contemplating making a second round of the plaques, when the nurse squeaked back.

"Some of the patients in maternity saw something," she reported. "A round, orange light moving along the ground. You can't talk to any of them now, of course. Tomorrow."

"Tomorrow's fine," I said. "Thanks very much." I pushed out through the glass doors. The rain was coming down like a second glass door. I sprinted back to my car, cursed at it until it started, and headed home. The car from Illinois was still in the same spot. No grandchild, I feared.

Karen had turned off the TV and was curled up on the end of the couch where the good lamp is, reading a magazine. "Mmmm?" she asked.

"Somebody floated a gizmo down Minnehaha Creek," I sighed.

"Glowing orange, of course. Flashing lights in white and green for a little added fillip, as the fashion pages say."

Karen put her finger on her place and looked up. "Sounds pretty elaborate," she commented. "Why would somebody do that on a night like this?"

I shrugged. "Friday. Friday is crazy."

"But why go to all that trouble for a rainy night? Save it for another Friday, why not? When the weather was better and more people would see it?"

"Friday is crazy," I repeated. I went out to the kitchen, got the last beer out of the refrigerator, and hooked off the cap. Karen wouldn't want any: she was off alcohol for the duration. Alcohol and a lot of other things.

She was still frowning when I went back. "Seems an awful waste," she said.

"It does seem funny," I admitted. "Probably burning a hole in somebody's pocket. Couldn't wait to get it launched." I sat down on the other end of the couch. "I'll go back tomorrow for my daylight look. Keep Prunella happy. All forms filed and in order."

Karen chuckled. She likes Prunella Watson, the head of CATCH. "Good idea," she said. "And now I'm going to bed." She shut the magazine and waddled away to the bathroom.

# II

KAREN'S father had a heart attack four days after we were married. It played hob with our honeymoon, as you can imagine, but for him it was hardly even an inconvenience as heart attacks go. Six years later the guy was healthier than he'd been since Karen was in kindergarten. He had a cardiologist who advised regular exercise and strict attention to diet, and since in Karen's book free advice from an expert is a bargain not to be passed up, I jog every day and have my two official eggs per week on Saturday mornings. (What Karen doesn't know about the company cafeteria won't hurt anybody.)

No eggs that Saturday morning. I told Karen I wanted to get an early start, which was true, and swallowed some scalding coffee and headed for the parking lot at Methodist Hospital. The lot was still pretty empty when I arrived, most of the cars clustered near the building, a few scattered farther out, toward the highway. I pulled the Ford to the edge of the lot near the road and got out.

The day promised heat later on, but in the early morning it was still cool and sunny. The blackbirds were singing *Conkaree!* in the cattails, just the way the field guides say. A thin mist rose off Minnehaha Creek and dissolved into the light breeze that had replaced last night's thunderstorm. I took a few tentative steps onto the mown grass beside the parking lot and stood on tiptoe to peer out over the rushes. Nothing to be seen, although I had the advantage of a decided dip in the terrain.

I left the car in the lot and walked along the side of Excelsior Boulevard to a little arched footbridge that crosses the creek. From the middle of the arch, I saw the first hard evidence of the hoax I was already convinced of: some soggy stuff that could have been tissue paper caught on a broken reed. Orange, of course. As expected. Curse all little high school girls with excitable boyfriends. I could have been home eating my breakfast.

Instead, I dodged an irate blackbird and crossed the highway. Clambering over a waist-high chainlink fence, a few twists of which had been bent down enough to make the operation somewhat less gingerly, I skidded down the bank to the stream. Here, thanks to the golf course of which it was a part, the grass was only ankle high and there was just a single spindly patch of cattails. I had no business climbing their fence, of course, but neither had whoever had pulled something like a canoe out of the brook recently enough to leave clear marks. Somebody wearing waffle-tread jogging shoes. I bent down and peered under the highway bridge. Nothing. No—not nothing: on the bank, close to the bridge and the little patch of reeds, a string of Christmas-tree lights was mushed into the mud. Green and white bulbs, one of them the kind that makes the whole string flash on and off. I dropped the string back onto the bank. Hardly worth taking a picture, and I'd forgotten the camera anyway. Prunella would have had a fit if she'd known.

Other than a hell of a long extension cord, I didn't immediately see how the lights had worked, but the rest was obvious: the "saucer," constructed of orange tissue paper on the order of the hot-air balloons that are a favorite of UFO fakers—I'd checked out one of those myself only a couple of summers ago—and lit from the inside, had been floated down the creek on a canoe. The power source—auto batteries?—would have been in the canoe, along with the hoaxer.

And the boy, Ken, seeing the UFO take off? Suggestion, most likely. I've investigated enough of these cases to see some otherwise very intelligent people believe some unlikely things against all kinds of physical evidence—and Ken's wit hadn't impressed me much. I left the string of lights lying where it was and climbed back up the bank.

In the car, I had a look at my well-worn map. Luckily, none of the crumbling folds crossed the area I was interested in. I spotted a couple of promising canoe-launch sites: Meadowbrook Boulevard, which runs back to the creek not far from the hospital, and Louisiana Avenue, which crosses the stream even closer. From where I sat, I could see the high retaining wall on the west side of Louisiana and the low apartment buildings above it that front on Meadowbrook. Louisiana, I decided, was more likely despite being four lanes wide. One of the near-

[ 16 ]

by company parking lots would have waffle-tread-jogger prints leading out of it, I was sure. As soon as I'd talked to a couple of maternity patients, I'd check them out.

I got out of the car and headed for the big pink brick building. The parking lot was beginning to fill up already, and my stomach was starting to grumble. I'd be quick, I promised my growling gut. Just long enough to establish in everyone's mind that this UFO had been identified as somebody's idea of a joke.

My CATCH card is an instrument of great power. It makes people laugh, and it opens doors. On the maternity floor, a plump, dark-haired nurse found a Mrs. Johnson willing to come down to the visitors' lounge and talk to me. Mrs. Johnson was older than I had expected, in her middle thirties, maybe, and her belly was still so big that I wondered at first whether she'd had her baby yet. She had, I discovered. A girl. I filed away the information that Karen might not come home from the hospital with her old twenty-two-inch waistline, and explained who I was.

Mrs. Johnson held my card as if she didn't quite want to touch it. "I'm afraid I'm going to disappoint you," she said. She had a shy, apologetic smile that reminded me of Karen's mother.

"Oh?" I prompted.

"That...*thing*...was no flying saucer. It was only some kind of a joke."

"Oh?"

"It looked like what you read about in some of these sensationalist accounts," Mrs. Johnson explained, her forehead standing up in little ridges. "But when I looked carefully I could see that it was mounted on some kind of boat, and somebody was steering it."

"It was on a canoe, I think."

She blinked. "You knew that? Then why come up here and ask about it?"

"Actually, I was hoping to stop any rumors that might have gotten started, by talking to people who thought they really did see a UFO."

The smile lost a lot of its shyness. "People believe what they want to believe, no matter what you tell them," she said. "My

[17]

roommate is trying to think of a suitable name for her son, one that will...oh, commemorate the occasion."

"Good grief," I said.

"She reads the *National Enquirer*."

"I see."

Mrs. Johnson tilted her head at me. "You're not what I expected," she said. "You seem almost..."

"Sane?"

"You said it." She had a lovely laugh. "Why are you mixed up with...this?" She flicked the corner of my card with her right index finger. "Committee for Analysis of Tropospheric and Celestial Happenings. How absolutely *grand!* How long did it take to dream that one up?"

"Search me." I'd fielded this one before. "It had to spell *catch*, see, because that's what we want to do. Catch one."

She laughed again. "Lots of luck! Sorry you couldn't snare this one."

"Oh, this is the easy kind. Catch them all the time," I assured her, and took my leave. One, two more stops, and eggs, here I come, I thought, and punched the elevator's down button.

"Are you Jamison?"

I turned around. The man was taller than me, skinny, in his late forties. He was wearing a white coat with a stethoscope stuffed into the right-hand pocket as if it were his medical degree. Behind me the elevator doors opened, waited while the guy eyed me, and closed. Impatient things.

"This is the last time you bother any patients or staff in this hospital, is that clear?" Doctor X rocked forward onto the balls of his feet and brought his heels down for emphasis.

"I don't think I bothered anyone," I said.

"That's for me to decide. Unless you have a personal reason for coming here, you are to stay out of the patient areas, is that clear?"

"Perfectly."

Doctor X reached past me with one long thin arm and stabbed the down button with his index finger. He pinned me with a gaze that would have done for fastening a butterfly to a specimen board and folded his arms. It was on the tip of my tongue to ask what his big beef was—I'd used, after all, maybe two minutes of a nurse's time and five, freely given, of Mrs. Johnson's. But I decided to let it slide.

I had other things to think about than arrogant doctors throwing their weight around. I smiled my nicest at him as the elevator door closed and proceeded to think about those other things. For example, and a peculiar one: whoever had gone to all that trouble to make a fake flying saucer didn't seem to have given much thought to what the gadget would look like from above.

I remembered reading somewhere that men who are searching for something seldom look up. And in fact, I once spent the better part of an hour hunting for a crying cat that turned out to be in the elm that used to be in front of our house. Where had I looked? Under parked cars, inside the garage, under the front porch. Still, with something as elaborate as my current unidentified floating object, you'd think the hoaxer would be more careful, because you couldn't not think of the hospital: it was the chief source of witnesses.

I was still puzzling about that when I walked past the Toyota with the Illinois plates.

I do not know why I stopped to look inside that car. Subliminal notice of the blood splashed on the windshield, maybe.

The guy inside was far beyond help. He was crammed down into the space in front of the passenger seat, but even from outside the locked door I could see the hole behind his ear and a lot of not-too-fresh-looking blood. A fly circled lazily above him and settled down again.

I leaned my back against the door of the car and told my stomach that since it was empty there was no point in even trying to throw up. I told my legs very sternly that they could too hold me up on my feet, and I shuffled back to the hospital building and up to the information desk and held on to the edge of the desk with both sweaty hands and said, "There's a dead man in a car in the parking lot. Call the police."

The woman behind the desk pushed her bifocals up her nose and stared at me through the tops of the lenses. "I don't believe I heard you correctly, sir," she said.

Sergeant Richard Chelon looked as much like a turtle as it is possible for a reasonably well-set-up young man to look. Something about his stillness, maybe, as if he were practicing to be a TV newscaster, or the way he blinked, slowly and infrequently—although to be honest I don't remember if I've ever watched a turtle blink.

"You say you don't know this man," he repeated for the nth time.

"I never saw him before this morning."

"But you went out of your way to look into his car."

"I explained that," I said. "I saw the car in the lot last night, when I was checking out this so-called UFO, and when it was still there this morning, I went and looked. I wish I hadn't, if you really want to know."

Sergeant Chelon explained that he didn't really care, that he saw no reason to believe anything I might have to say, and that what I wished or didn't wish made no difference whatsoever to the established order of the universe—all with just one of those slow blinks.

"Look, I'm an old buddy of Mack Forrester's," I said again. "Why don't you check with him?"

"Mack's off today," Chelon said, the first information he had seen fit to divulge. He was so surprised at himself that he blinked twice.

My stomach grumbled.

"Tell me about this hoax."

I went over it again: how Mack had called me, how I had trailed the two kids back to the parking lot, how I had decided it was a hoax—the weather, the description, the location—how I had gone back for physical evidence that morning.

"And where were you when this thing was floating down the creek?"

"Me!"

"You."

"I—I'm not sure. On my way home from Hopkins, I think. With my wife."

"Going past the hospital, here?"

I had gone past the hospital, as a matter of fact, although it hadn't occurred to me before. Excelsior Boulevard is the quickest route from downtown Hopkins to my area of Minneapolis.

"I guess. I didn't see this thing, though."

"No." Chelon waited. I had nothing else to say, but I began to have the panicky feeling that I should say something. Anything.

"Why do you think somebody would pull a stunt like that?" the sergeant finally asked.

"Search me. If it had been mine, I'd have saved it for a clearer night."

"What if you couldn't?"

"I don't get it," I said. "Why couldn't I?"

Chelon blinked.

It was well past noon when I walked into my kitchen, and by that time I was ready for breakfast.

"Where've you been?" Karen asked. "I thought you'd be back by nine! I was getting worried."

"A long story, honey."

"Well, take your head out of the refrigerator and tell me about it," she demanded, snatching the carton of eggs from me.

"I found a murder victim."

Karen stared at me, much as Sergeant Chelon had. Very slowly, she sat down at the kitchen table with the carton of eggs clasped in both hands. "Was it very bad?" she asked.

"Not after the first shock." Leaving out the details the police had been so interested in, I told her about the man in the car. She got up and started to fry a pair of eggs, blinking at the quarter pound of margarine in her hand as if she didn't quite know what it was.

"You see what they're thinking, don't you?" she blurted, once she had broken the eggs into the pan.

"What?" I was already salivating.

"That the UFO was arranged to cover up the murder. To distract people's attention, so no one would notice that the man was being shot."

"Karen, guns make noise."

She thought that over. "There are such things as silencers, aren't there?"

"So our magician not only misdirects attention, he makes noise silently?"

"You're not being fair."

"No. You could be right," I acknowledged. "It does make more sense than a joke on a night like last night."

Karen shook the frying pan, watching the eggs. "Do they think you did it?"

"Me!"

"Well?" She set the eggs, the whites just set, the yolks still deliciously runny, in front of me. "What do they know about you?"

I looked out the back window, at an oriole that was picking at the halved orange Karen had set out on the bird feeder, and back at the eggs. Revolting-looking things.

"Maybe you ought to call Mack Forrester," Karen suggested.

"Later." I forced myself to eat the perfect eggs. Hell, I protested to myself, I had never even seen that guy until this morning! Why should anyone think I'd kill him? And that I'd work up a kludge like that to do it? It was a little insulting to be suspected of such a half-assed stunt, when you thought about it.

Before I got around to calling Mack, he called me. "Listen J. J. Be careful what comes out of your mouth," he warned me. "You're in *some* kind of trouble! I hope you've got a good attorney."

I put the phone down and went over to the Warner's in the Miracle Mile and charged a garage-door opener on my Visa card. I figured Karen might need it in a few more weeks, and I'd better get it installed before Sergeant Chelon decided what to do next.

So I installed it, and then I took a shower, mopped a wad of brown hair out of the tub, worried a little about premature baldness, and discovered that there was nothing on TV I wanted to watch.

That, pretty much, was Saturday.

# III

"Joe?"

Karen had spread the Sunday paper out on the kitchen table, so that she could read and knit at the same time. The sun shining through the east window through her hair gave her a halo, a bright curly outline that shifted as she turned her head.

"Yes, angel?" I said. She made a face.

"Does the name David Streich sound familiar to you?" She gave the last name the full German pronunciation.

"I don't think so. No." I went back to the sports page, where I was reading about the iniquities of the Twins and Calvin Griffith, as described by an employee thereof to a sarcastic reporter. I noticed vaguely that Karen had risen and moved away from the table. "How about getting me some coffee while you're up?" I asked.

"Get it yourself; I'm busy." She was in the study, soon to be a nursery, not in the kitchen. I heard a file drawer slide shut.

A moment later Karen appeared at the near end of the hall with a folder in her hand. "David Streich," she said. "Three years ago, he sent up a bunch of those tissue-paper balloons with the candles in them, remember? One came down out in Plymouth and started a grass fire that spread to some building."

"Oh, him," I said. "He pronounces it 'Strike,' as in 'I'll strike you dead if you ever do another thing like that, young man.'"

"Joe, that's not funny. He is dead."

"You're kidding."

Karen motioned me into the kitchen after her and wordlessly pointed to a picture in the newspaper.

Like most newspaper pictures of tangled wreckage, this one wasn't very clear, but it was clear enough so that it didn't take much to imagine what had happened to the driver. I felt sick. The kid would have been eighteen, and he was bright and easygoing, the kind you know will go places and make no enemies doing it. Even I, investigating a prank of his that cost me a lot of time and trouble, had thought more than once that I wouldn't mind having a son like Dave Streich.

"Friday night," Karen added. "Coincidence?" She looked up at me expectantly.

"I'm a little dense this morning, Kay," I said. "You'll have to spell it out for me."

"What if he was your hoaxer?"

"Dave?" I pulled a picture out of the back of my mind: a blond kid with a kid's version of his mother's teasing grin, shocked at what his lighthearted stunt with the balloon had done. "I can see the saucer," I said. "But David would never kill anybody. And some guy from Illinois?"

"He didn't, of course," Karen said impatiently. "Couldn't, if he was in that boat with the saucer."

"Canoe."

"Oh, all right. Canoe. You *are* dense this morning! Can't you see that that trick took two people, one to guide the UFO down the creek and one to do the killing?"

"That's true." I read the caption under the three-column picture. No details, just the name and the day, and the location, on Highway 100 at 36th Street. Bad intersection with a somewhat unexpected light. Might even have been the accident I drove past on my way to Methodist to check on the UFO. For some reason I didn't care to examine, I hoped not.

"You think he was killed to keep him quiet?" I asked.

Karen nodded. It seemed ridiculous for her to be standing there in a flowered housecoat that didn't quite meet over her belly, discussing murder.

I shook my head. "How would the killer get him to go along with a deal like that? David was basically a good kid. Just a joker. He might jump at the chance to run a fancy saucer like that, but not on a wet night. He'd want the biggest audience he could get and a big laugh afterward, not a dead man."

She spread her hands out, palms up. "You're the investigator, not me."

"UFOs, Kay. Not murders. I call airports and find out what flights were up. I calculate the position of Venus in the sky. I call agencies and find out if they had an advertising plane flying, check the weather-balloon schedules, stuff like that."

"And climb down banks and find waffle-tread footprints and old strings of Christmas-tree lights."

"So?"

"So, what about this kid? Did he have shoes to match those prints?"

"You're asking me?"

"Don't you want to find out?"

I looked back down at the newspaper and began leafing through it, looking for a report on the murder of the man from Illinois. "Karen, I can't bother his mother right now. Maybe in a few days."

For one thing, Anne Streich would bother me. She didn't look anything like old enough to have an eighteen-year-old kid, and she had a slow, crooked smile I really didn't want to encounter with Karen off-limits until after her delivery. But maybe she wouldn't have that smile, under the circumstances.

I kept turning pages, scanning the columns bottom-to-top so I wouldn't skip anything. Near the back of the second section, a picture looked up at me—a studio portrait of the man I had last seen jammed into a space several sizes too small for him. Victor Amant. A lively-looking face, a sideways glance, a thin mouth gathered higher on the left than on the right, dark hair, light eyes. I'd never have recognized him without the story beside the picture.

"He looks like a ladies' man," Karen remarked.

It occurred to me that Karen might be feeling our strictures too. The guy in the restaurant, the picture in the paper... "Says here he's a manufacturer's rep for a little Japanese office-machine company. Kyoto Copiers. Works out of the Chicago office. That explains why he was here, I guess, but you'd think he would fly."

"Which reminds me," Karen said. "You're going away tomorrow—do you care what I put in your overnight bag?"

"Anything decent." I reread the four inches of story. Kyoto Copiers. Never heard of them. Lots of companies I've never heard of.

I turned back to the picture of Dave Streich's MG. Karen

could be right, I thought. In that case, if only for the boy's sake —or the sake of his memory—it might be worth looking into. I got up and picked up the phone and dialed.

"Hi, Joy, it's J. J. Jamison," I said to the light voice that answered. "Is Mack there?"

"Sure. Just a sec."

More like a few minutes, but then Mack's deep voice came on the line. "What's up, J. J.?" he asked, sounding cautious.

"Mack, I'm looking at a story in the paper about a car crash Friday night. The Streich kid."

"God, yes. That was a mess."

"You know he had a history of UFO hoaxes?"

"No, I didn't. So?"

"I'm wondering if he had anything to do with Friday's gadget. It kind of fits with something he did a few years ago."

Mack was quicker than me. "He was hired, you think?"

"Something like that."

Silence on the other end of the line, long enough for me to pull the phone cord out full length and investigate the coffeepot, in which I found only a brown sludge that covered half the bottom. "J. J., it won't fly. That's all I can say."

"Some old buddy you are. Can't you tell me what time the accident was, at least?"

"I guess." Mack didn't sound very enthusiastic. "You could get that anywhere. A little after eleven, it was."

"After the saucer."

"Hell, yes." Now he sounded annoyed. "You were there when the call came in."

"Oh." I remembered the robot talk. "Anybody check out that car? See what kind of shape it was in before the crash?"

"What for?"

"See what caused the accident."

"J. J., the kid had been drinking, and he hit the back of a semi at the 36th Street light. Do yourself a favor and forget it. Even the insurance company won't think twice about it."

"Still…"

"Look, J. J., fixing up a car to kill somebody is fine if it works, but you got to use something like a bomb; otherwise, as a mur-

[ 26 ]

der method it's not too reliable, check? You're a great guy, but you've got your job and I've got mine, and do I tell you how to do yours?"

"I'm not—" I stopped. No point in having old know-it-all mad at me. "I mean, all I'm trying to do is give you some info. You know, looking for an A in citizenship."

"Okay, you got it." Another silence. "Don't go talking to any cops but me unless they ask, check? Stay cool, J. J."

Karen was back at the newspaper when I hung up. I washed out the coffeepot and set it up for another brew before I left the kitchen.

"Joe?" she said, as I headed back to the couch and the sports section. "They have a memorial notice for David Streich. Visitation this afternoon, at that place down on 50th Street, where Roland Eskew was?"

"You want to go?" I asked, surprised.

"No, but I thought you might."

I settled into the couch and shook out the sports section as the coffeepot harrumphed into life in the kitchen. "I'm not going to any funeral parlor to ask about waffle-tread joggers, I'll tell you that."

"I meant," Karen said, her voice heavy with disgust, "that you might want to pay your respects."

"I'll think about it," I said, but as soon as she put it like that, I knew I would go.

So at three-thirty that afternoon, I was driving ye olde lemon south, sweating into my navy-blue suit. On a Sunday, after church hours, there was plenty of space to park. I cracked the windows in a forlorn hope of preventing the vinyl seats from melting in the June sun and climbed the broad steps to the funeral parlor—or funeral home, as they call it these days. Inside, beige walls, a red carpet with a leafy pattern like something out of my great aunt Susan's front bedroom, and enthusiastic air conditioning.

I was directed to the right room by a youngish man filled with professional sorrow and concern. The sleek mahogany coffin was closed. Three people huddled on the chairs at the opposite end of the room: David's parents I recognized, and the blond

guy with them looked somewhat familiar. A couple, young people, came in just behind me and ambled toward the three. I
looked at the flowers. Besides the white roses on the coffin, just
two arrangements so far. Not that every petal in Pasadena on
New Year's Day would have been compensation enough.

Uncomfortable, as who wouldn't be, I hovered on the fringe
of what was now a growing group until Anne Streich spotted
me. "Oh, it's...I'm sorry...Jamison, Mr. Jamison, isn't it? J.J.—
I remember! How sweet of you to come."

I mumbled something about regretting the circumstances,
while her husband looked confused.

"The UFO man," she said. "From David's little escapade."

I was fairly sure Harry Streich had paid a bundle for David's
little escapade, but he managed a polite nod. A far cry from the
hearty laugh I remembered, with more than a little secret glee
over what his son had done.

The blond man turned to talk to someone. "My brother-in-
law," Anne Streich said, gesturing at his back. "A bad year for
both of us, so far." She lifted an elegant handkerchief to her
eyes and blotted underneath the lower lashes: a fakey-looking
gesture, but the tears were real. "Last March, my sister died.
And now my son."

"I'm sorry to hear that," I said. I wished I hadn't come. "I was
very sorry to read about David."

She smiled, a taut little smile. Even she didn't know what to
say, I realized, for all her expensive deep blue dress and careful makeup. For the first time I'd ever seen, she looked her age.

I took a deep breath. "You know, there was a saucer hoax Friday night," I said, very quietly.

Her eyes flew wide open. "No. Any...damage?"

"None. Hardly noticed. But if anything odd should come up
regarding David, could you call me?"

She gave me a curt nod and turned slightly away.

"Mrs. Streich..."

"Anne," she corrected, but her voice was distant.

"This is an odd question, I know, but could you tell me if David
by any chance might have owned a pair of waffle-tread joggers?"

"I don't keep track of his shoes, J. J.," she said. "You will sign the book, won't you?"

I nodded, answering the question and acknowledging the end of the conversation. "I really am sorry," I said. "I liked your son. A fine boy, really."

She smiled and looked past me. The door of the funeral parlor opened, sending a shaft of sunlight across her fine-boned face. On it was a look of intense worry.

I left.

The street was hot, dusty despite Friday night's torrents, and the vinyl seats of my car were soft enough to make me glad I'd left the windows open. I stood outside the driver's-side door, letting waves of heat escape, and wondered what I was getting into.

To save Karen the drive, I took a cab to the airport in the morning.

Now, I like computers. But I never was a hacker, and hundred-hour work weeks are not something I look upon with the slightest degree of eagerness. I do my job, and I do it well, but I don't sign up for extras. So I'm the guy they send to ride herd on the subcontractors, and that's why I was on my way to Chicago that day. An overnight quickie.

It did occur to me that there was a bit of irony to be mined from the situation: for all I knew, I'd shared a few planes with the manufacturer's rep from Kyoto Copiers. But by the time I got to O'Hare, I was absorbed in my job and had pretty much forgotten about Victor Amant.

I picked up my rental car and headed east on Interstate 90 just as if I didn't have an extra care in the world.

# IV

ON Tuesday evening, the 747 sliced through stacked-up clouds and burst through the bottom just over Lake Harriet. A sure sign of thundery weather: jets roaring over my backyard are a more reliable forecast than anything I've ever seen on the Twin Cities' weather-happy television. We touched down like a first kiss and rolled toward the gate with the flight attendant imploring us to remain seated. I pulled my bag out from under my seat, released the seat belt, and poised to sprint. Karen would be waiting for me at the gate.

But she wasn't. The waiting area was completely empty. I walked slowly up the long, bright corridor toward the terminal, not wanting to miss Karen if she'd been late and was one of the few people hurrying in the other direction. The plane had landed a few minutes early, and our flock of people moved up the slight incline in a loose knot.

I spotted Mack Forrester before I spotted my wife. No trick to it: that fair head sticks up six inches over the rest of the crowd, far enough that I could see him scratching his moustache. He raised a hand when he saw me, and I saw that Karen was at his side. I slid diagonally through the crowd, slipped behind the desk where a cop was keeping people out of the boarding area, got tangled in the crowd again, and was cast up at Mack's left hand.

"I'm honored," I said.

"I'm supposed to check that you really are on the plane." Mack didn't smile, and neither did Karen.

I looked from one to the other. "What is this?"

"Chelon's got a bee in his bonnet about you," Karen said.

I jumped a little at hearing her refer to the man with such hostility; I hadn't even realized she knew his name.

"J. J., I don't know what's going on," Mack said. "You got to understand Chelon just made detective last winter, and we don't get all that many murders to investigate." He shook his head. "So...I dunno about Chelon. Trying to show the big boys from Minneapolis he's just as good at his job as they are, maybe."

"Let's go get a drink and you tell me about it," I suggested.

"I'm, uh, kind of on duty," Mack said, glancing down at his orange-striped sport shirt and brown slacks.

"Coffee shop, then. Karen can't drink anyway. We can have some iced tea."

"Okay. I don't have much to tell, though," Mack said. "You got baggage to claim?"

I lifted the bag in my hand. "Just this."

"That's something, anyway," Mack said, like a man the world had descended upon. I saw Mack glance back at the security guard and glanced back myself, but the guy was only reading a book.

"How come you couldn't come to the gate?"

"Hijack threat," Mack said. "Shut them up tight. Ticketed passengers only. I don't know why a smart hijacker wouldn't buy a ticket, but it's not my baby, thank God."

We moved slowly away from the concourse, toward the coffee shop. On the main terminal floor, there's a lounge area for people who want to smoke—Minnesota has a clean-indoor-air law, meaning smoking isn't allowed in the more general public areas—and Mack ducked his head like a tailback with the ball under his arm and headed for the cluster of plastic seats.

"Hey, what about our iced tea?" I asked.

"In good time, J. J.," Mack said. "I'm sorry. I got to search your bag."

"Search my bag?" I glanced at Karen. Her mouth was tight, and she was nodding slightly.

"I got a warrant," Mack sighed.

"More Sergeant Chelon," Karen said. She had pulled her hair back behind her ears. I saw that she hadn't put any earrings in, making the dimpled holes of her pierced ears look terribly vulnerable. I wanted to kiss them and make them all better.

Mack held out one of those big, hairy hands of his. I passed him the bag, and he heaved it up onto one of the seats. "What have you got in here, rocks?" he asked.

"Paper."

Mack had the bag open. He groaned. "I'm supposed to read anything I find," he said.

"It's all company stuff, Mack," I said. "I don't know if I even have the authority—"

"*I* have the authority," he interrupted, tapping a paper that stuck out of his back pants pocket. "I just don't have the stamina." He picked up my Monday shorts and shook them out, smoothed out my Monday socks with a grimace, gave my Monday T-shirt a shake, fingered the pocket of my Monday dress shirt, peered into the pockets around the edge of the bag. He eyed the documentation and the listings I'd brought from the subcontractor. "Company business, you swear to me?"

"Stack of Bibles, Mack. They've all got our name on them."

He flipped open the covers and nodded. "Okay. Don't tell Chelon, huh?" He shoved everything back in the bag, pulled out my shaving kit and looked into it without much interest, replaced that, and zipped the bag up. "Let's go get that iced tea."

When we were settled at a nonsmoking table with three glasses of iced tea, and a doughnut for Mack, I said, "Now, what gives?"

"You didn't go down to the station and sign your statement," Mack said. "That's the first thing."

"Chelon said, at my convenience. I had to go out of town. It hasn't been convenient."

"Yeah, well, he doesn't buy that." Mack drew a line with his forefinger from bottom to top of the iced-tea glass, in the condensation, and touched the resulting drop of water to his tongue.

"Jeez, Mack, if he meant right away, why didn't he say right away?"

Mack shrugged and took a sip of tea. "Cops always mean right away. Then there's this Victor Amant."

"The guy who got killed. I saw the story in the Sunday paper."

"Right." Mack sighed. "You told Chelon you'd never seen him before."

"I hadn't."

The look I got was as pitying as the one my sixth-grade teacher used to give me when something obnoxious turned up on her desk chair. "Turns out he's been dealing with your company for three years. Makes four, five trips a year up here just to see your guys."

"Hell, Mack, it's a huge company. He could come every day and I might not ever see him. I don't even know nine-tenths of the people in my own plant, and this guy probably spent his time at headquarters."

"How do you know?" Mack ate the middle out of his lemon slice and made a face.

"I don't know it. I figure it."

"Yeah, well, do yourself a favor and don't spring any figuring on Chelon."

"He'll think you met the guy at headquarters and got to know him that way," Karen said. She looked tense and worried, and that worried me.

"Has he been bugging you?" I asked.

"He wasn't happy with you for going out of town without letting him know," Karen said.

"He didn't ask me to," I protested.

"It's a murder case," Mack explained. "You're supposed to know these things."

"Without being told?"

Mack shrugged.

"What's the matter with you guys? You think because I investigate UFOs I'm into mind reading, too, or what? Astrology, maybe? Tarot cards?"

"Calm down, Joe." Karen put her hand on mine and squeezed. "Now that you're back, just like I said you'd be, everything'll be okay."

"I hope," Mack said.

"You look tired," I said to Karen.

"I've had a rough time," she said. "Cops, reporters…"

I knocked back the rest of my iced tea, wishing it were bourbon. Beer, at least. "Let's get out of here," I said.

The echoing terrazzo floor of the main terminal was nearly deserted. A few bored-looking men in uniforms matching their airlines leaned on the long ticket counter, too far apart for conversation. Above us, the flags of all the nations hanging below the gridwork of the ceiling looked as dispirited as I felt. The automatic door hummed open, and Mack marched through.

The air, as I'd anticipated, was soggy and hot. In the distance, a rumbling noise that could have been a plane or thunder. Only one cab at the stand, the driver resting a magazine on the steering wheel. Downstairs, there might be more cabs, but it was Tuesday night, the graveyard shift of the week.

We crossed drearily into the parking lot. Mack, it turned out, had driven Karen out in his own car. He unlocked it, and I tossed my bag into the back seat. Karen got in the front, and I slid in back behind her, not happy at the arrangement, but Mack has an old Honda Civic, and very pregnant ladies don't fit into the back seat very well.

Nobody said much while Mack steered us down the ramp to the exit. I offered to pay for the parking, and he said, sounding none too pleased about it, that the department would pay.

"I can put it on my expenses, Mack," I said.

"Forget it."

He tucked his receipt into his shirt pocket and swung the car onto the exit road, heading east to link up with the crosstown highway. We made the wide curve around old Fort Snelling, and I thought again that it would be fun to go to one of their Fourth of July celebrations, with the fort the way it had been in the last century. It occurred to me that if Mack could get his parking paid for, the trip was official, and I wondered if I'd ever have the chance to watch the soldiers fire their muskets. I didn't ask.

Lightning flashed in the west as we made the turn for the crosstown, heading right into the storm. "More damn rain," Mack said, reaching for the wiper control. "Never seems to quit. I got a lawn I could lose a kid in."

The wipers squealed across the windshield. Not even Karen, who's usually bubbling when I come back from a trip, seemed to have much to say. We hissed along the highway without more than half a dozen words among us. At Xerxes, Mack left the crosstown. "J. J.?" he said, pulling up to the traffic light. "There's a funeral for that kid tomorrow morning. Do yourself a favor and stay away from it."

"For Dave Streich? How come so late?"

Mack shrugged, barely visible in the dashlights.

"Mack, the kid was kind of like a friend."

"Don't go," he repeated.

"Why not?"

"Chelon's going to have the ceremony watched, I bet," Karen said. The edge of her cheek turned green as the light changed. "I'm beginning to see how the man's mind works."

Mack turned north, up Xerxes, without saying anything. "You've got to go to work tomorrow anyway," Karen said. "So you couldn't possibly go to the funeral."

"Yeah," I agreed.

So Chelon was having Dave Streich's funeral watched. That could only mean that he thought there was a connection between Amant's murder and Dave's accident after all. Maybe even some shred of evidence. And it had to be Mack that had put him on to it.

I smiled in the dark. Wheels within wheels, Mack trying to keep me out of trouble without messing up the murder investigation. Touching loyalty. Or was he just hoping to pick up some more information?

Mack waited in the car until we had hustled through the rain and opened our front door. I turned and waved, and he drove away.

Karen dropped onto the couch in the family room and rubbed her face with both hands. "I hope this all blows over in a hurry," she said. "I guess now that you're home I ought to plug the phones back in."

"That bad?"

She nodded. "That Chelon, he's persistent."

I went to the funeral anyway, of course.

# V

On a wide, low rise southwest of Minneapolis sprawls a pancake of a building that is the first enclosed shopping mall ever built in the United States.

The town that built it is Edina, long *i* and accent on the second syllable, and the shopping center tells you two things about the town: that its weather, winter and summer, is just as severe as what the rest of the Twin Cities area has and that somebody there has the money to do something about it.

Contrary to popular rumor, not everyone in the town of Edina is a majority stockholder in a Fortune 500 company. The Minneapolis papers have even reported a few AFDC families living in Edina from time to time. The Streichs are not among the latter, nor are they among the truly wealthy. Their solid-looking brick-and-slate house, a mere four times the size of my own, sits on a largish but not enormous lot in the Morningside area, close to the Minneapolis line. I'd been there several times while I was investigating the tissue-paper balloons that had caused young David so much trouble. I wasn't headed there now, of course, but to a nearby church.

I parked, grateful for the shade of a large elm, and walked up the steps to the church. My sport coat wasn't quite appropriate for a funeral, but it was muted and dark, so I hoped it would do. I could hardly wear my navy-blue suit without arousing Karen's suspicions, though, and I didn't want to upset her.

The interior of the church had that aged-wood-and-stained-glass look described so well in English novels. Everything but the accompanying chill and musty smell was duplicated here by the liberal application of hard cash. Not many people had come to commemorate the short life of David Streich: other than his father, balding head erect in the front row, his mother, hiding under a dark blue straw hat, and what I took to be other assorted relatives, there were fewer than a dozen people, most of them about the dead boy's age. The coffin rested at the end of

[ 36 ]

the aisle, under a purple cloth, and I saw the blue straw hat tilt toward it and away several times as we waited for the minister to appear.

At last he arrived and said the few prayers of the Office for the Dead, and the coffin was carried back down the aisle. Chelon lurked in the shadows of the last pew, I noticed. I hoped he'd gotten his money's worth.

I was standing near the aisle, and Anne Streich glanced at me as she followed the little procession out of the church. Her eyebrows rose, and she smiled, a small, sweet smile. I nodded once, not knowing what else to do. And it was over. By the time I headed down the steps, not more than twenty minutes after I'd climbed them, the hearse was already pulling away from the curb. My car was still cooling in the barely shifted shade of the elm tree. As I pulled away from the curb, I could have sworn I heard somebody yelling my name.

I got back to the cubicle I share with Pedersen, known to Karen as the Great Dane, little more than an hour after I had left. Pedersen lifted his shaggy fair head and nodded at me with the unfocused look of a man in the middle of a puzzle, so I just sat down at my desk and went back to dealing with the phone messages that had accumulated during my two days away. I dialed somebody called Jim Hudson first, a company number I didn't recognize.

"Purchasing," a woman said.

"This is Joseph Jamison," I said. "I'm returning Jim Hudson's call." He'd called three times, I saw as I sorted through the call slips. Hudson, Hudson. I shook my head.

"Jamison?" The brusque voice wasn't one I knew. "Are you the guy that sicked the cops on me?"

"Cops! I don't think so," I said. Pedersen glanced at me and went back to work. "Do I know you?"

"I sure as hell don't know. Who are you?"

"I'm an engin——Oh!" Light dawned. "Is this about that murder in St. Louis Park?"

"Victor Amant, yes. I never would have believed that jackass could be more trouble dead than alive."

Pedersen's chair squeaked as he turned to look at me. He had a quizzical look on his long face. "I found him," I explained, both to Hudson in Purchasing and to Pedersen.

"Lucky you. Did you send me this Sergeant Chelon, too?"

"No, he got there on his own," I said. "Why?"

"The guy comes over here and takes all my appointment books for the last six months, which gave my secretary such a case of heartburn she had to take the rest of the day off, shows me your picture—"

"My picture!"

"Have I ever seen you in the company of the deceased and like that. Have I ever gone out with you and Amant, are you connected to Kyoto Copiers in any way, et cetera, et cetera."

"Good grief," I said. A mild exclamation under the circumstances; I felt it was deficient in some way. Pedersen was now leaning forward in his chair with his forearms resting on his knees, head tilted as he listened.

"Not that I haven't had a drink or two with Amant myself," Hudson continued. "And I bet my secretary's had more than that. Trust him to get himself killed. Why couldn't he do it in Chicago?"

I didn't know what to say, so I didn't say anything.

"Well, I can see you aren't talking," Hudson said. "Sorry to take up your time."

"That's quite all right," I said, but he had hung up without waiting for politenesses. I looked at the receiver to see if it would tell me more, but it didn't, so I put it back in its cradle.

"It sounds," said Pedersen, "as if you have gotten yourself into what might be called a stereotypical American situation."

"Stereotype for who?" I asked. "I don't know anybody else who goes around finding bodies."

"Whom," Pedersen corrected. "For Europeans, of course. Not that we Scandinavians aren't just as bloodthirsty as anyone else. Care to tell me the tale?"

"Let me finish these up." I skipped over the calls from Chelon —I knew what he wanted. Maybe on the way home. The next slip was from somebody named Justin Hugbetter.

"Hugbetter," I said. "Sounds familiar. Can't place it, though." Pedersen said nothing, so I shrugged and dialed.

"KRAT-as-in-television-TV News," said a sultry female voice.

"This is Joseph Jamison. I'm returning a call from Justin Hugbetter."

"Yes, Mr. Jamison. One moment, please."

While I waited KRAT-TV's idea of a moment, I covered the receiver and asked Pedersen if he knew anyone named Hugbetter at Channel 7 News.

He shook his head. "I watch ABC, myself. I like this Ted Koppel. Do you suppose the man could have been educated in England?"

"You're asking me?"

Just then the phone clicked at me. "Jamison?" said a velvety male voice. I had a vision of an avalanche of caramel and molten chocolate bearing down on me. "This is Justin Hugbetter. Too bad you didn't return my call right away."

"I was out of town."

"Well, you're stale news now, so I'm sorry, no interview. Let me know if you find any more bodies."

"Sure," I said, and stared at the phone some more. It didn't have any more explanations than it had had on the last call, so I hung up, well behind Hugbetter. What made him think I *wanted* an interview?

"Now," said Pedersen. "The tale of your adventure."

Almost lunchtime anyway. No point in trying to call people who were probably out, so I tilted my chair back and recounted the saga of Friday evening and Saturday morning, to Pedersen's gloomy delight.

Half an hour later I bought a bowl of purported chili in the cafeteria, put it where it claimed to belong, and returned burping to my desk. Pedersen was gone. A couple of cubicles away, I could hear a heated discussion about the proposed architecture of a new computer. Not my group. The phone rang.

"Is this Joseph Jamison?" Squeaky Midwestern male voice, not one I recognized.

"That's right."

"You are the owner of a light blue Ford Fairmont, license number FEJ-972?"

"That's right." A little bubble of uncertainty formed in my chili. "Something wrong?"

My caller hung up. I looked at the receiver, shook my head,

and cradled it. No complaints, no concern of mine, I decided, and went back to work.

I got about an hour's hard labor in before the phone rang again. Pedersen was back by then and picked it up. "It's for you," he said, handing the receiver over. "Your lovely wife."

"What's up, Karen?" I asked.

"Joe, have you had any funny telephone calls?" she asked. She sounded a little panicky.

"Why do you ask?"

"Somebody called here a little while ago and asked when you were expected home. I told him, but he wouldn't leave his name. I—I know it's dumb, but it bothers me."

I looked at her smiling face, taped to the gray plastic wall beyond my desk. "Probably an insurance salesman," I said. "I wouldn't let it bother me if I were you."

"I...wouldn't an insurance salesman leave his name?"

"Look, honey, just don't worry," I said. "Lock up the house if you're nervous, and when I get home, the guy will probably call back and try to sell us central air conditioning. Okay?"

"Okay." I chatted with her for a few more minutes, until her voice lost its anxious edge, and hung up.

"Back in a couple of minutes," I told Pedersen, and got up. I found my way through the maze of cubicles to a window overlooking the parking lot and squinted against the sun to spot my car. It was just where I'd left it. It looked normal from my second-floor vantage point, and nobody was hanging around it. I tried to remember whether I'd locked the doors, decided I had, and went back to my desk.

"Everything is all right with you, yes?" Pedersen said.

"Yeah, I think so."

"The child has not decided to arrive early?"

"Karen didn't mention it, if it has."

Pedersen grinned and swung back to his desk. "She'd mention it," he assured me, out of the experience of having fathered five children in seven years.

I decided not to work late to make up for the time I'd taken off that morning. I figured the company owed me for the night

I'd spent in Chicago anyway. So I joined the outward flow at four-thirty, unlocked my car and stood aside to let the solar energy escape, exchanged a few remarks with a guy who used to be in our group but got himself assigned to another project when ours leveled off. Eventually, I got in and backed out of the space. There was some fluid on the pavement where my car had stood, not much. I didn't remember seeing it there when I parked: another ailment the dealer would greet with a glad hand, no doubt.

"You could be replaced with a bicycle," I told the old lemon as I shifted into first. Not a bad idea when I thought about it: a bicycle ride in the cool morning would be great, winding along by the lakes. The ride home in the hot afternoon would be hell. Everything balances out in the end.

At the end of the line of parking stalls I lifted my foot off the gas, and the car slowed obediently. But when I stepped on the brakes, nothing happened. I was going only about five miles an hour when I hit the red Chrysler.

The girl driving the Chrysler came out like an explosion. "What happened?" she demanded. "You weren't looking, or what?"

"I saw you," I said.

A couple of people took their hands off their horn buttons and got out of their cars.

"Was it too much trouble to put your foot on the brake," the girl demanded, "or are you trying to get rid of that junker, or what?"

"The brakes failed."

"The brakes failed," she repeated. By now her hands were clamped on her hips and her left foot was tapping rapidly. "You think that's going to go over with your insurance agency, maybe? This is a brand-new car!" she added, flinging a hand toward the Chrysler. "I've had it a month, and look!"

Her name tag identified her as an engineer. "Let's just trade information and get out of here," I said.

"Good idea," agreed one of the bystanders.

"You work and work and save and save, and finally you get to buy a new car and some asshole in a clunker comes along and smacks it up, and all the sudden it isn't new any more," the girl complained.

"Look, I'm sorry," I said. "I couldn't help it—my brakes went out."

"If you would maintain your car properly, that kind of thing wouldn't happen."

"Yeah." I wrote the name of my insurance company and my license number on the back of one of the CATCH cards and handed it to her.

"I knew it," she said. "I had to get hit by a nut."

I was writing her name and the license number of the Chrysler on the back of a second card and didn't bother to answer. Horns were honking again. A couple of guys volunteered to help me push my car to the side, and after a while the girl gave me her driver's license to copy, took it back with a glare, got in her car, and drove away.

My "clunker" had eight months of a three-year loan to go and was scarcely neglected. Sometimes Karen and sometimes I had spent long hours in the dealer's grungy lounge waiting for the old lemon to be readjusted one way or another. I managed to pry the hood loose from the remains of the grill and had a look under it.

Somebody had taken a bright nick out of my brake line just past the master cylinder. I went back into the building and called, first the insurance company, then a tow truck, and then the police.

Karen met me at the front door. "Joe, what happened? Why the cab?"

"I had a little accident with the car," I said. "Nothing very serious, don't worry. But it has to be fixed before we can drive it again."

She was a little pale, looking very pretty in a light yellow smock, with a yellow-and-white scarf pulling her light brown hair back. "David Streich's mother is here," she said. "I thought you'd be home much sooner, and she's been waiting."

"Never rains but it pours," I said. I followed Karen into the family room, where Anne Streich sat on the plaid Herculon couch like a fire opal in a setting that had come out of a gumball machine.

"I couldn't help overhearing," she said. "I hope no one got hurt?"

"No."

She closed her eyes and let her head rest on the back of the couch. "That's good," she said. "J. J., you told me to call you if something unusual came up."

"Has something unusual come up?"

I let myself down onto the edge of the armchair from Levitz that had looked so nice until I'd seen the inside of the Streichs' house, and that had been three years before.

"First, I have something to confess. I told you an almost lie." She opened her eyes halfway—to gauge the effect of the statement, I guessed. "About Davey's shoes."

"He did have a pair of waffle-tread joggers, then?"

Her eyes closed. "He was wearing them when he died."

I heard Karen's shocked intake of breath. I could see why Anne Streich had denied knowing about the shoes, I thought. The question must have seemed like a thunderbolt to her, coming out of the blue.

"I'm sorry," I said. I was: I'd hoped Dave's joggers were the more common corrugated kind, to rule him out.

She smiled briefly, eyes still closed. "Also, I—I was given a package by the funeral director. He said I might want to have my husband look at it right away. So of course, I opened it myself."

Karen and I both nodded.

"It had Dave's…effects in it. Including seven crisp, new hundred-dollar bills that were found in his shirt pocket."

Karen's mouth and eyes went round. "Seven hundred dollars!" she exclaimed.

"I know it doesn't seem like much," Anne Streich said, "but it was a lot for Dave. He's been trying to pay his father back for the damages he caused in that fire—you know parents are liable for any damages their children do?"

"Yes, I think so."

[ 43 ]

"It's not an awful lot, really, but Dave is—was—a responsible boy. I know it may not have seemed like that to you, what with those balloons."

"Just a prank," I said.

She didn't seem to have heard me. "I cannot imagine where he got that seven hundred dollars! I've been racking my brain all afternoon. He did have a job, but I can account for almost everything he earned from that, and he can't get at his trusts until he's twenty-one. So where…?"

She sat up convulsively and put her face into her hands. "But he'll never *be* twenty-one!" she cried. Karen moved onto the couch and laid a tentative hand on her shoulder. After a moment, her voice muffled, Anne said, "I suppose he might have done that hoax you talked about, and been paid for it."

"It's possible," I said cautiously.

"But why would anyone pay so much for a joke?"

"I can't imagine." I looked up at Karen, who was shaking her head slightly. She thinks people should face whatever comes. "I wouldn't worry about it," I said.

"If he was involved in something illegal, drugs or something—what would I do?"

"I don't think it's very likely," I said. "Drug dealers don't get paid in brand-new money, as far as I know." True enough: what the hell do I know about drug dealers?

"I've got the money with me," Anne said. "I don't want to leave it around, somehow." She looked up at me with her round, bloodshot blue eyes. "I don't know what Harry's going to say."

My stomach chose that moment to grumble about its unfed state.

"Oh, you'll be wanting your dinner!" Anne said. "How inconsiderate of me!"

"Not at all," I said staunchly. "I asked you to call me, and you were kind enough to come around even though it must be very distressing for you."

"I don't know. I feel lost. I'm so confused. First Paula, now David…"

"Paula was your sister?" I asked, remembering her comment in the funeral home.

"Yes. Of course, she was no better than she should be, but she was my sister."

I looked to Karen for enlightenment, but she shook her head. "I—forgive me, I'm a little confused."

"Oh! Of course. You didn't know. All our friends do, and I tend to think... She drank herself to death."

"She what?"

"Quite literally. Got so drunk she just never woke up."

"Isn't that rather odd?"

"Not really." Anne had her face under control; she turned on an earnest look that might have been real. "There was even an autopsy. It showed a weak heart. But it was a shock to us, even so."

"I'm sure it was."

She began gathering herself together: purse, gloves, presence of mind. "I'll be going, and you can have your dinner," she said.

I wondered. I didn't smell anything cooking, but maybe the refrigerator had a salad in it. "Mrs. Streich?"

"Anne," she corrected, smiling at Karen.

"I know this is an impertinent question, but I'm a little bothered by something. Someone who was at the scene of Dave's accident said he'd been drinking. Is that likely?"

"I don't think he can have been drunk," she said. "I talked to a friend of his who was with him at Shakey's until...oh, twenty minutes before the accident, and he said Dave'd only had one beer." She shook her head, her mouth in a tight line. "And to think I was having dinner right next door! Life's little ironies," she added, getting to her feet. "If anything else comes up, I'll let you know. Though I really don't think Dave could have done your hoax if he was at Shakey's, could he?"

"Not possibly," I agreed. "But if you wouldn't mind giving me the name of Dave's friend, I think I'd like to talk to him."

She frowned, revealing a depth of line in her forehead that wasn't otherwise apparent. "I don't remember," she said unconvincingly. "Bob something. I can look in the book and see if he signed."

She meant the book they kept at the funeral parlor, I realized, in time not to ask. "I'd appreciate that," I said. "No big rush." I followed her to the front door and watched her walk across the street to the cream-colored BMW I had unaccountably not noticed when I came in, and shut the door only when the glossy car had pulled away from the curb. "What's for dinner?" I called to Karen.

She met me halfway through the living room. "Nothing. I was just about to start it when Anne Streich showed up, and I didn't like to say, 'Sit there and amuse yourself; I've got to cook,' so I figured, well, we can always go out for pizza. But now... after what she said, I don't have much appetite for pizza, and with no car..."

"I'll jog over to the Tom Thumb and pick up something quick," I said. "No sweat."

Karen moved over to the living-room window and pulled the sheer curtain slightly aside. "She's very... elegant, isn't she?" she said wistfully.

"Anne? She is indeed," I agreed. Then I got it. "But it's you I love," I added. "And you're looking splendidly pretty, in my book."

Karen grinned and stepped close, and I leaned over to fit the big curve of her belly into the hollow of my own and kissed her thoroughly. Now, who says I'm always so dense?

# VI

Six o'clock, and the afternoon was still sweltering. I decided not to jog.

At first I was tempted to take Karen's bike, because of the baskets slung on each side of the back wheel, but the seat on mine is set higher and I've grown to like the little rearview mirror Karen put in my sock last Christmas. So when I saw that my old backpack was hanging, for some inexplicable reason, over the handle of the lawnmower, I took the extra two minutes to wrestle my own bike out from behind Karen's.

Being in motion helped. The breeze dried and lifted the short hair at my hairline as I headed for Xerxes Avenue in one long downhill swoop. I felt cool for the first time in hours. If the tan Volkswagen Rabbit was behind me then, I didn't notice it. It appeared in my mirror, annoyingly close, when I had made the turn onto Xerxes and the hill was against me.

"Jeez, mister," I grumbled aloud, over as close to the parked cars as I could get. "You'll run me down if you crowd me any more." At the 44th Street light, the Rabbit had to stop, so I took advantage of a lack of cross traffic and just kept going, cursing inconsiderate drivers. Illegal as it was, I didn't stop for the stop sign at the next corner either, just made my right turn and pedaled the five short blocks to the Thumb.

The Thumb was icily air-conditioned and smelled as usual of perchloroethylene from the dry-cleaning establishment that shares the building. Also as usual, the doors were bracketed by small mobs of pop-drinking kids. I picked up a six-pack of Old Milwaukee just in case, piled two cans of sardines on top, grabbed a loaf of whole-grain bread, and passed up a buy on strawberries. A jumpy kid in a red dust coat rang up my purchases. I packed them into the backpack myself, shoved the fistful of change into my pocket, and negotiated the teenage blockade.

The Tom Thumb lot is built on a side-to-side grade. The Rabbit had pulled up next to the first light standard, facing downhill, toward the store. I didn't think anything of it, of course. On a hot day there's a lot of activity in late afternoon, as people decide they can't stand to cook after all, and for all I knew here was another lazy citizen out for sardines. So I was whistling as I unlocked my bike from the railing that keeps inattentive drivers from plunging through the store's plate glass and slung my backpack up on my back. I headed uphill, toward the back of the lot, to shortcut down the alley back to Xerxes.

I was about ten yards into the alley when I heard the Rabbit revving behind me.

He—or she—was much too close for comfort. I pedaled faster, hoping to gain some distance, but the Rabbit just speeded up. It dawned on me that the Rabbit was *trying* to hit me! I dodged as best I could with nowhere to go: chain-link fence clotted with weed trees to my right, the high wall of Saint Thomas's school to my left.

The Rabbit hit a pothole and nipped the reflector off my back fender. I lurched, recovered, and skimmed the edge of a cluster of deep craters. The Rabbit slowed for the potholes, but it kept coming.

I pedaled. I didn't look back: the little rearview mirror showed clearly enough that the scrap of Rabbit it reflected was gaining again.

I popped out onto Xerxes to the music of screeching brakes from the cross traffic, crossed both lanes, and made my left turn, past a low office building. Nowhere to go that the Rabbit couldn't follow. I labored up the few yards of the hill. The light was against me, and this time there were no holes in traffic to give me a break. Right, onto 44th Street, then. Pray that the light stays red, the traffic keeps up, and the Rabbit can't make it.

The Rabbit made it. Throat aching, lungs protesting, a stitch in my side, I pedaled for all I was worth. The Rabbit was right behind.

Somebody going the other way sounded his horn.

I saw an infinitesimal break in the traffic to my left and ducked through it down a side street. Behind me, a satisfying screech as the Rabbit braked.

[ 48 ]

Ten seconds later he was behind me again, and I knew I had had it. I rode up somebody's driveway and along the side of their garage, ignored the startled shout of some guy flipping hamburgers on a grill, boosted my bike over a low fence, and rode on down the driveway beyond. Now I was on the next street over, and the Rabbit would have to go around the block. I liked that so well that I did it again, glad some people chain up their dogs.

Five minutes later, I was home. I didn't see the Rabbit, but I took no chances on stopping to put the bike away: I just ran it onto the lawn behind the house and got myself behind a locked door as fast as I could.

"What did you get?" Karen called from the family room.

"Sardines." I could hardly get the word out.

"Sardines! I had sardines, you nut!" Karen came into the kitchen. "What on earth...? Joe, sit down. How come you're so out of breath?"

"I was riding pretty fast," I gasped.

"In this heat? Joe, you're crazy. You know better than that."

My lungs were coming back to normal. Maybe Karen had something, with her exercise program. "I thought you were hungry," I said.

"I am, but I'm not going to starve to death in an extra five minutes." Karen poked into the backpack and pulled out the sardines and the bread. "Want them on toast?"

"That would be nice."

"You didn't get any lettuce."

"I knew there was something I forgot," I said. "Should I go back?"

"Not worth it." She dropped a couple of slices of bread into the toaster. "Why don't you take a quick shower while I get this ready?"

"Good idea."

In the bedroom, I half stripped and reached for the phone. "Joy?" I said, keeping my voice low. "It's J. J. Can I talk to Mack?"

"He's on duty, J. J.," Mack's wife said. "And he's mad at you about something—did you know that?"

[ 49 ]

I groaned quietly. "Joy, ask him to call me when he gets home."

"It could be after midnight, you know. Could he call you at work tomorrow?"

"Listen, I have to talk to him." I listened for a second but heard nothing to suggest that Karen wasn't still in the kitchen. "I don't care if it's three o'clock when he gets in—tell him to call me right away, okay?"

"Life and death?" she asked, laughing.

"Exactly."

I hung up on a sobered Joy Forrester and finished taking off my clothes. Five minutes later I had sluiced off the sweat and climbed into shorts and a T-shirt.

"I've got a lemon," Karen said, as I walked into the kitchen. "Would you like a thin slice of lemon on your sardines, instead of lettuce?"

She wasn't looking at me: she was looking at the sardine from which she was carefully removing the backbone. One end of the scarf that held her hair back was caught lightly into the neckline of her dress. The yellow dress was reflected in the white fronts of the kitchen cabinets like sunshine. My wife, spreading sunshine in my kitchen, and twice in the past few hours, somebody had tried to kill me! I tried to say no thanks to the lemon, but I couldn't get the words out.

"Joe?" She turned, the knife in her right hand. "I said, would you like some lemon?" Her head tilted. "Are you all right?"

"Yeah," I got out. "I'm fine."

She peered at me. "You've overexerted yourself in this heat. Your face is all red."

I went and collapsed on the couch, and in a couple of minutes Karen brought me two slices of toast with sardines topped with paper-thin slices of lemon, with a neat border of sliced garden tomato, the first of the season.

I ate the toast and did what I could to make the house secure: locked the doors, pulled out the stops that keep the windows from rising more than five inches, put a new battery in the smoke detector as I'd been meaning to do for weeks. I turned on the porch light. Security isn't something I worry about too often, but if Karen thought anything was odd, she didn't say so.

Some cop from St. Louis Park called, and I promised him that I'd come in the next morning before work without fail and sign my statement. I thought about unplugging the phone.

It could be a long evening. And was. Nothing on TV I wanted even to pretend to watch. As the least of the evils, I turned on something the Twins call a baseball game, crossed my fingers, and allowed myself just one of the 3.2 beers I'd bought. Finally the ten-o'clock news came and went, Karen and I went to bed, and I could lie in the dark staring at the dim ceiling and listening to the window fan and waiting for Mack to get done with his damned job and call back.

The digital clock had just clicked its orange numerals from 1:16 to 1:17, when the phone rang. I caught it before the ring was finished.

"Okay, J. J., what is it?" Mack asked.

"Hold on a sec, Mack," I whispered. "I want to take this in the kitchen." I set the phone down on the night table and slipped out of bed without waking Karen, groped my way to the kitchen in the dark, and picked up the other phone. "That's better," I said. "I don't want to wake Karen up."

"Yeah, well, get on with it."

"Mack, I'm in trouble."

"You're telling me! You still haven't signed that damn statement, you know that?"

"I know, I know. It slipped my mind, is all."

"J. J." Mack's voice was pained. "You don't forget things like that. This is a murder case, remember? You want Chelon to bring you in?"

"Well, someone called a while ago, and I promised to come down and sign it first thing in the morning. But I don't have my car anymore..."

"Take a bus. A 17 drops you right at the door. How come you went to that funeral, after I told you to give it a miss?"

"I told you, Mack—the kid was somebody I liked. Now, will you listen to me?"

"Chelon wants to swear out a warrant," Mack said. "All he

lacks is motive and opportunity. Do yourself a favor and go sign that statement. How come you don't have a car?"

"That's what I'm trying to tell you, damn it. Somebody tried to kill me!"

"When?"

"That's better. This afternoon. First, he called me at work, checked that I owned a blue Fairmont. Then, when I started for home, I didn't have any brakes and I smacked up some girl's new Chrysler."

"Anybody hurt?"

"No, it was just one of those parking-lot deals. I lost my grill and bumper; she lost her rear fender. Seven, eight hundred bucks, probably."

"Not good, J. J."

"You're telling me! Listen. I looked under the hood, because I remembered a puddle on the ground where I'd been parked, and there was a shiny new nick in my brake line. Looked like somebody went after it with a file or a hacksaw."

"Oh, hell. That's worse."

"I told you, somebody's after me. Then, after I got home, I biked over to the Tom Thumb on 43rd, and on my way home somebody tried to run me down."

"What kind of car?"

"Tan Rabbit."

"You call the cops?"

"And tell them what?"

"You got the plate number, didn't you?"

"No."

"What the hell's the matter with you, J. J.? You got any idea how many tan Rabbits are running around?"

"Look, I was busy trying not to get run down, okay?"

"Man or woman?"

"Driving, you mean? I'm not sure. A man, I think."

"You think!" Mack seemed to have been rendered speechless. I padded across the dark kitchen, stretching the phone cord as far as it would go, and tried to see into the backyard. Nothing moving out there, anyway.

[ 52 ]

"J. J., listen," Mack said. "Keep this one quiet, understand?"

"No."

"I mean, don't tell anybody. Listen, that kid's car? He had a nick in his brake line too. When he once got onto Highway 100, he didn't have a chance. Soon as that light turned red, he was dead."

"Well." I sagged against the counter. "I guess I was lucky."

"Yeah, I believe that. Chelon won't. Chelon will think you're just smart."

"I don't get you."

"He'll think you staged your accident yourself. Camouflage. You and all the other ducks on the pond."

"What about the Rabbit?"

"A tan Rabbit! No license, no description of the driver—you got any witnesses?"

"No," I admitted. "It was mostly in the alley."

"Look, I'll do what I can, but you're in Minneapolis, and that's not my turf. Keep your eyes open."

"Sure," I said despondently. I hung up and felt my way back to the bedroom, hung up the other phone, and eased into bed.

Karen sighed. "Don't you think I had a right to know, Joe?" she asked.

"I didn't know you were awake."

"Would it have made any difference if you had? Dammit, I thought we had a *partnership*. What kind of marriage is it when you can't even tell me somebody's threatening your life?"

"Karen, I'm sorry."

"It was all even as long as I was working and we were saving for the house, wasn't it? Is that what it takes to be a person? Money?"

"Karen, I just didn't want you to worry," I said.

"I'm a big girl now, Joe," she said. "I'm going to be a mommy pretty soon."

"That's just why I don't want you upset," I explained.

"I'm only pregnant, dammit, not coming apart. It's not like I had a terminal disease."

I turned on the lamp beside the bed. Karen was lying on her

[ 53 ]

back, staring at the ceiling, and tears had run down the sides of her face into the hair at her temples. I reached out, and she turned to me with a sob.

"It'll be all right," I said, stroking her hair. "I'll get this all straightened out, and everything will be okay." She smiled, a little disbelieving smile, and I knew she was asking herself the same question that had popped into my own head: how?

# VII

If the sun takes pleasure in its accomplishments, it must have been ecstatic when it rose the next morning to find that the air had not lost any noticeable heat overnight. I called a guy I know slightly, who works in the same plant I do, to cadge a ride to work. Karen wasn't any keener on my going than the guy was on driving half a mile out of his way to pick me up, but I figured I was as safe at my air-conditioned desk as anywhere, and the farther I was from Karen, the better. I sure didn't want any attempts on me to misfire and involve my wife!

"You have a bicycle, have you not?" Pedersen asked, when I mentioned my arrangements for getting to work. "Why not ride it to work? This isn't so very far. In Europe, we do this all the time."

"Last time I rode my bike, which was about fourteen hours ago, somebody tried to knock me off it," I told him. "With a car."

"Indeed?" His eyebrows rose. "This is getting rather exciting, isn't it?"

"For you, maybe."

"You would prefer not to be involved?"

"Right."

"Understandable. Understandable." Pedersen rocked in his chair for a minute or two, sucking thoughtfully at his lower lip. "Tell me once again, in greater detail, this entire story," he said. "Perhaps we can determine who is doing these things."

"The police think they know."

"Indeed?"

"Me."

Pedersen laughed. "That *is* serious," he admitted. He sucked at his lip some more. "Yes. You had best tell me this story again."

So I told him everything I could remember, from Friday night's call from Mack right down to my conversation with Mack the night before. I left out Karen's reaction. Pedersen looked as if he had fallen asleep.

"That's about it," I said.

[ 55 ]

"Ah." He opened his eyes and sat forward. "First, this doctor. You haven't told me his name."

"The one who threw me out? I don't know it."

"He did not have a name tag on his pocket?"

"I don't think so." I tried to picture the man, but apparently my memory had lost a few bits. I couldn't get any impression of a name tag. Stethoscope in the right-hand coat pocket, yes.

"That's odd," Pedersen mused. "Usually, they have their names on them." He said it as if he had come upon an unidentified specimen in the Fall Chrysanthemum Show at the St. Paul Conservatory. "What did he look like?"

I should have remembered that Pedersen probably knew Methodist's entire obstetrical staff. "Tall, skinny, forty-odd. That honey-colored hair blonds get when they're older."

"Ah, yes." Pedersen passed his hand over his own darkening hair. "I think I know that one. There was something, some trouble about when my Margritte was born. A woman treated poorly. A botched abortion, perhaps? But it was all of no great consequence, I think. All turned out well in the end."

"So that lets him out," I said.

"Not necessarily," Pedersen said, with a narrow-eyed smile. "Doctors have lives as do the rest of us, and into them some motive may come. His behavior was somewhat peculiar, was it not? And the scene would be both familiar and convenient to him."

"True." I wondered if I should mention the doctor to Mack. Seemed like damned little evidence to bother the man about.

"Then there is also the possibility that he is not the doctor I think, but another," Pedersen continued. "Perhaps not even a doctor at all, but just a man in a white coat with a stethoscope in his pocket." Pedersen lifted his eyebrows, for him the equivalent of a triumphant grin.

"Hunh-unh," I said. "You don't learn to act like that without eight or nine years of training. And how would he get away with walking around the hospital like that? The nurses know who's supposed to be there and who's not. Any doubt, and they'd have Security up there in two seconds."

Pedersen pulled at his chin, which was already long enough,

and abandoned the doctor. "What about this man from Purchasing who called you? What do you suppose he wanted to know?"

"What it was all about, I guess."

"Or perhaps he wished to convey something," Pedersen said, still working at his chin. "Well, we have not much to go on. And the daily routine calls, after all."

So I tossed him for coffee and lost. "Come and get me if Karen calls," I said.

I bypassed the closest coffee machine, which makes an even worse brew than most, in favor of one that produces a semipalatable cup. I'm ashamed to have to carry such sewage back to Pedersen, who is something of a gourmet, but he drinks it uncomplainingly enough.

"A woman called." Pedersen took the steaming plastic container with his usual dubious look at its contents.

"Karen?"

"Not Karen. She will call back in ten minutes."

"She didn't leave her name?"

"Not this one," Pedersen said. He gave me a knowing look that made me wonder what one does for a sex life when one's wife spends half her life either pregnant or recovering. One finds a more liberal obstetrician, I'm told, but I can't swear to it. Pedersen set his coffee down on the far corner of his desk, as if unwilling to acknowledge that it belonged to him, and turned back to his work. I turned back to mine. Well, I looked at it, anyway.

Five minutes later I went out to get myself a second cup of the evil brew and missed my mysterious female caller again. You'd think that the heartburn the coffee brings on would be penance enough for drinking it.

About ten, she called a third time, and this time I was there to take the call. "Is it Mr. Jamison, finally?" she asked. The voice seemed quite young, but that can be deceptive: people still ask my grandmother if they can speak to one of her parents. I admitted I was me.

"You don't know me," she said.

"No," I agreed.

"I think I only want to tell you my first name. It's Linda."

"Hello, Linda." Strangest come-on I'd ever heard. She sounded almost as nervous as if she were being chased by a mad Rabbit.

"I'm...I was a friend of Victor Amant's."

I looked up at Pedersen, who had turned around and was listening unashamedly. "Oh?"

"I wondered...I wondered if you'd meet me for lunch somewhere. I...I have some questions..."

I waited, but she had run out of words. "If you're wondering what he might have had with him when he died, I'm afraid I don't know," I said.

"No, no. Nothing like that."

"Where did you get my name?" I asked. "And how did you know I worked here?"

"Why, your name was in the story in the Monday-afternoon paper. Didn't you see it? They said that you work for this Committee for Analysis of whatever it is. CATCH, anyway. So I just called the main library and asked them for the address of CATCH headquarters, and then I called Boston and got your number at work from them. But of course, I don't know where that is."

"You're very enterprising," I commented.

"Well, don't you see? I have to talk to you. I don't know anybody else, and I don't know what to do." A small silence. Then she asked, in a very tiny voice, "So, could you meet me for lunch? I'll pay."

"Well, I don't have a car just now," I temporized.

"You don't?" Again, she was silent for a moment. "I hope it wasn't...um...tampered with?"

"Why do you ask?"

Another pause. I wanted to wind her up with a big key in the back, like those dolls they have in comic strips and nowhere else. "Because that's what happened to Victor. Last spring. Somebody put a nick in the brake line of his car and covered it up with a piece of tape. So it wouldn't leak until he got on the freeway, he said. Victor, I mean. Only it—the tape—came loose right away, and he could stop the car with the handbrake." She paused again, but I had nothing to say. After a moment she went on, "That's when he gave me this stuff. Oh, was I scared! But Victor was just furious; he said that dumb trick was really going to cost somebody. It was an Avis car, you know."

I heard a jingling noise. Pedersen was shaking his car keys to get my attention. "I think I may be able to borrow a car," I said. "Where do you want to meet?"

"Well, I don't know where you are."

*And I'm not going to tell you,* I thought with sudden caution. "What would be convenient for you? I can go almost anywhere."

"You know, I don't think this is such a good idea after all," the girl said. "Not if somebody's been messing around with your car." She hung up.

I looked at the receiver, got no more explanation from it than ever, and replaced it. "Cold feet," I said to Pedersen.

"You aren't bold enough, Jamison," he said. "But don't despair. She will surely call back." He shoved his keys into his pants pocket and swiveled to his desk. "After all," he pointed out, "she has shown great determination to speak to you, so far."

I had something else on my mind. I wasn't going to get any work done anyway, I rationalized, so I might as well satisfy my curiosity. "Back in a few minutes," I told Pedersen. He shrugged, deep in his work.

Out in the blazing sun of the parking lot, I stood for a few minutes trying to remember where I had parked the old lemon the day before. The first place I tried showed no sign of anything spilled on the asphalt, but the second showed clear traces of the puddle of brake fluid under the front end of the Chevy somebody had parked in that spot that morning.

And yes, there was a little twist of dirty strapping tape, poking out under the edge of the Chevy's left rear tire. I teased it out and carried it back to drop on Pedersen's desk.

"What's that?"

"Half of a murder weapon. Not terribly effective, fortunately. Worked only one time in three."

"Like guns." Pedersen nudged the blackish scrap of tape out of his way with one well-groomed forefinger and picked up his pencil. "Wrapped around your brake line, no doubt," he said. "No wonder it's so unreliable."

"Maybe he'll get lucky with the Rabbit," I said, sunk in gloom.

To which Pedersen blandly made a reply so obscene that I forbear to burden this narrative with it.

We worked for several minutes in as much silence as one of these cubicles with its five-foot-high walls can ever afford. "How did he get into your car?" Pedersen asked abruptly. "Doesn't the hood latch from inside?"

"Oh, my own damn fault. I left the windows open a couple of inches because of the heat. He must have stuck something in and pulled up the door button."

Pedersen considered this. "How would he catch hold of the button? Something sticky?"

"It's not like your car," I explained. "It's got sort of mushroom-shaped tops on the buttons. Piece of wire or a noose of string would do it."

"Piece of pie," Pedersen said.

"Cake."

"Éclair, for all I care." We dropped back into silence, and I actually got a little documentation done.

I was standing at the snack machine wondering whether the cafeteria's version of chow mein had settled well enough that I could chance the taco-flavored tortilla chips or whether I should stick with stale shoe-string potatoes, when Pedersen came looking for me.

"It's that girl who called this morning," he said. "This Linda?"

"Here?" I exclaimed.

"On the telephone."

I let the machine keep my quarters and hurried back through the maze to my desk. "Yes?"

"Mr. Jamison?" The voice sounded even younger than it had earlier that day. "I've been thinking, maybe I was too hasty this morning. I've got all this stuff and I've got to figure out what to do with it. Could you meet me for dinner, instead? I'll still pay."

"My wife's expecting me home for dinner," I pointed out. Pedersen chuckled.

"Oh, you're married." She sounded odd: I couldn't figure out whether it was disappointment or relief. "Couldn't you explain to her? Is she the jealous type?"

"No, but—"

"Please, Mr. Jamison. It wouldn't take long, and you could even just have a cup of coffee or something with me and go on home for your dinner."

"Well…"

I could hear her take a deep breath. "There's a good place on 50th Street. Near France. Do you know Edina well at all?"

"Yes, but—"

"Just for a few minutes." She paused. "If you don't have a car, you could just say the bus was late. If she's the jealous type."

"She isn't. Really. But I'd rather—"

"*Please*, Mr. Jamison!"

I looked at the picture of Karen on my wall and made that small shoulder wiggle that constitutes both apology and plea for forgiveness. "Okay," I sighed. "When should I be there?"

"Could you make it by five?"

"Five?" I sighed again. "It'll be going some, but I think I can make it."

"Oh, thank you!" she gushed. "Oh, you don't know how grateful I am. I really need to talk to somebody." We finished making arrangements, and I hung up.

"Where is it you need to be at five?" Pedersen asked.

"A restaurant in Edina."

"I'll give you a ride," he offered. "With, of course, a string attached. I find myself most curious about this young woman. I would like to hear all about this rendezvous when you come in tomorrow. The young lady's anxiety transmitted itself all the way to my desk." He grinned. "I am most intrigued."

"I bet you are." It was on the tip of my tongue to offer to let him take my place, but on second thought, he just might agree to do it—and my own curiosity was strong enough to resent the idea.

Now to get up the nerve to call Karen. Better to plunge straight in, I told myself, and dialed for an outside line.

Karen's "Hello" sounded a little faint.

"Kay, honey, I'm sorry. I'm going to be a little late," I said. "I have some catching up to do and I'm not sure how the busses run."

"Okay." She sounded odd.

"Are you all right?" I asked.

"I think so," she said. "The heat's getting to me, I guess. It must be ninety-five in here."

I remembered the hot sun in the parking lot. "Did you remember to pull the shades down?"

"Of course I did," she said, apparently lacking the energy even to sound annoyed. "But since they cut that big elm down across the street, the sun just beats in the living-room windows."

"Well, stay as cool as you can," I told her. "I won't be too late."

"Okay. I'll just fix a salad, so it will be ready whenever," she said. "Goodbye."

I hung up feeling guilty, but it was already too late to change things: I had no way of getting in touch with Linda, and I didn't want to stand her up. Sighing, I left Pedersen muttering Scandinavian imprecations at the computer terminal on his desk and went back through the maze to the snack machine.

Which, with the aid of one of my co-workers, had eaten my fifty cents.

# VIII

FRANCE Avenue into downtown Edina was stop and go at that hour of the afternoon, but Pedersen didn't seem in the least distressed. He piloted the Volvo with the first two fingers of his left hand, his left elbow hanging out the window, and used his right hand to gesture as he talked. I found myself hanging on to the edges of the other bucket seat with both hands.

"I have searched the personnel files," Pedersen was saying. "This Hudson—"

"How did you get into the personnel files?" I asked.

Pedersen looked pained. "Jamison, as a reasonably competent engineer, must you ask? It is a simple time-sharing system, after all, and the architecture is not so difficult to master. I deduced the code—"

"I thought you were working awfully hard this afternoon," I muttered.

"Not hard—steadily," Pedersen corrected. "Now, about this Hudson in Purchasing. He is six feet, one inch tall, weighs 183 pounds, and has blue eyes. They don't record hair color on driver's licenses, so I can't tell you that."

*Good God,* I thought. *Has he been into the state's files too?*

"He has an adequate salary, somewhat higher than yours, two wives, one former and one current, no children. Yet his bank account—"

"Steadily," I said, "wins the race."

Pedersen looked confused, which gladdened my heart. "I'm not sure I..."

"Aesop," I said.

"Oh, yes. The—what's the word?—fables. As I was saying, his bank account shows unaccountable drains. Perhaps he has been doing some extracurricular purchasing."

"Possibly," I said. Pedersen had probably been the type of little boy my mother didn't want me playing with, I thought suddenly. Attractive and amoral.

"Or perhaps paying this Amant for something. He said to you that he had gone drinking with the man."

"How do you know that?"

Pedersen turned his head and delicately touched his right earlobe. "I have excellent hearing," he said. I wished he'd watch the road, but maybe he had excellent eyes on the side of his head. I didn't ask.

"How did you know where his bank account was?"

"Simple. He has his paycheck automatically deposited." Privacy is a thing of the past in this country. There are a lot of Pedersens around.

"Maybe he's got a savings plan," I suggested.

"Indeed he does. Seventy dollars a month into the credit union, five toward savings bonds, forty for the stock-option plan, twenty into the pension plan—"

"Stop!" I said, putting my hands over my ears.

"You would be well advised to do likewise," Pedersen continued earnestly. "Especially with the child coming. He will need an education...."

"I have a mortgage."

"Limited liquidity," Pedersen sniffed. "Why don't you investigate some of these new savings plans? The individual retirement accounts look good."

"I don't plan to retire for thirty years," I said. "At least."

"May I remind you of the fable of the grasshopper and the ant?" asked Pedersen. "Is that another of Aesop's?"

"This," I said firmly, "is where this grasshopper jumps out. Pull over, will you?"

"How will you get home?"

"Walk," I said. "It's less than two miles."

"See you tomorrow, then." Pedersen grinned and gave me a thumbs-up sign. I reminded myself to think up a wild story for his entertainment and slammed the car door. The Volvo pulled straight into traffic, to the consternation of an elderly woman in a rusty gold Duster. I waited for the light to change and crossed the street.

Linda X. had told me she'd be wearing a dark blue linen suit, not that I'd know linen from tar paper, and a blue floral-print blouse. She needn't have bothered. I was twenty minutes late, and she was standing close to the glass door of the restaurant peering out, her high, pretty forehead creased twice down the middle, her mouth slightly open, and the strap of her big leather purse twisted so tightly around her fingers that her flesh stood out in ridges on either side.

"Are you Linda?" I asked.

"Oh!" She stared at me. "I expected someone a little less, uh, conservative."

CATCH does that to people. Sometimes I call it Catch-22, but only for my own amusement. "I'm in disguise," I told her solemnly.

"Yes," she said, sounding a little breathless. "I guess you'd have to be."

I revised my initial estimate of her age downward by five years, which made her nineteen.

A tubby hostess asked us if we wanted smoking or nonsmoking seats. I was about to say non, when Linda hurriedly said, "Smoking, please." The hostess gestured with her plastic-coiffed head for us to follow her. I stepped back to let Linda pass and got a whiff of the same hair conditioner Karen uses, a lemon-honey-scented concoction that makes her smell cozily like an old-fashioned cough remedy. I followed Linda toward the table with another pang of guilt.

While I got us supplied with sandwiches and iced tea, Linda dithered over whether she was going to tell me why she had enticed me into a restaurant when I had a perfectly good home to go to with a perfectly good dinner waiting in it. The restaurant she had chosen wasn't the best for her purpose: it came equipped with a hovering waitress, and the tables were set close together. Though they hadn't filled up quite yet, I was almost as much a part of the intimate conversation going on behind me as I was of the one I was having with Linda. More. They were talking.

"Well," Linda said, when the waitress had plunked the sugar bowl down and gone away. She drew a deep breath, with the air of a condemned man awakened for his last breakfast. "I suppose you're wondering."

I only nodded, since my mouth was full of bacon and sliced turkey on caraway toast. No lettuce here, either.

She opened her enormous purse and stared fixedly at its contents. After a moment, she pounced in with one hand and pulled out a pack of cigarettes, which she put beside her plate without removing one. "I ... Victor ... we were special friends, you know what I mean?"

I nodded.

"Nobody knew. Nobody. It had to be that way, you know? Victor had that kind of job."

Manufacturer's rep for a Japanese office-machine company. He could have patronized every prostitute on Hennepin Avenue and nobody would have given half a damn. I nodded again. Victor, it seemed, had been a very careful man. I wondered how a man that careful had ended up stuffed into the bottom of his own car in an empty parking lot.

"And besides," Linda said. Her fingers caressed the cigarette pack some more. I wished she'd take one out and get it over with. "Victor's wife was an invalid. He couldn't, you know, have sex with her. But it would have killed her to find out that he was unfaithful." She rubbed at her left eye with the heel of her hand. Either waterproof mascara really is, or those lashes were all her own. "I didn't get to see him often, of course. He was only in town a couple of times a month." She stopped and examined her iced tea.

"I understand," I said. Holy cow, talk about feeding a line! This Victor had used the undercover job *and* the pathetic invalid wife, and this chick had bought them both. Reprehensible, I told myself sternly, but I couldn't repress a sneaking admiration for Victor Amant, nonetheless.

"That's why, when he had this vacation— Did you know him?" she asked suddenly. "Personally?"

"Me? No."

She sucked in her lips and put the cigarettes away. "How did you happen to become involved?"

"I was out there investigating a report of a UFO in the swamp next to the hospital, and I noticed his car, Friday night. When the car was still there the next morning, I looked inside."

"So he did go there instead! I wonder why." She looked around the restaurant and shivered slightly. "See, we had a date Friday, and he never came. And he didn't answer his phone at the

[ 66 ]

motel. I didn't know what to think. And then Sunday, I saw in the paper…" She stopped again, bit her lips, wiped the other eye. "Excuse me," she said.

"That's all right."

She picked up half of her sandwich and put it back down. "I don't know… So there was a UFO, too? They didn't have that in the paper. I wondered why they put that in about the Committee for whatever."

"There wasn't really a UFO," I said. I wondered how much to tell this girl; she had turned fairly pale. "It was just somebody's idea of a joke."

"How…weird."

I took a deep breath and plunged. "I think—the police think—it was supposed to distract attention from, uh, what was going on elsewhere in the lot."

She surprised me. "Victor being killed, you mean," she said, with a brief nod. "But he was shot, wasn't he? Wouldn't somebody have heard?"

"There was a thunderstorm going on around then. And the car was closed. Or the killer might have used a silencer on the gun."

She picked up the iced tea and took a tentative sip, then set it back down precisely in the center of the saucer. That was the first thing she had eaten or drunk. I felt like a boor as I finished my sandwich.

"I need some advice," she said. "I called you because…well, because you're an investigator. You know all about these things."

"UFO investigations aren't quite the same thing as police investigations," I said cautiously.

"Close enough." She nodded, as if to convince me, or maybe to convince herself.

"Something wrong with the sandwich, dearie?" asked the waitress.

"No, it's just fine." Linda put both hands protectively over the sandwich, and the waitress ambled away to bother somebody else.

Linda blinked. "Where was I?"

"You want advice," I reminded her.

[ 67 ]

"Yes." Again the deep breath. "I told you about the car. Early in March, that was. After that, Victor left a package with me. I opened it up and looked at it, after I found out he was dead, and I can't figure out whether the police should have those things or not."

"Why don't you take them over and ask?"

"Oh, no, no," she said hurriedly. "No, I can't do that. It would all come out about Victor and me, and if my mother ever found out…"

I wondered if she was even nineteen, though she certainly looked every day of it—and more, now.

"That's why I thought I could give them to you and you could give them to the police, if you thought it was something they should have."

"Why me?"

"Like I say, you're an investigator too, and then you work for this CATCH—and that seemed like a—a—an omen. Like you could catch whoever did this, you know?"

"What kinds of things are in this package?"

"It's an envelope, really. There's some papers. A Xerox from some book about murder investigation that says how you could use dry ice for a perfect murder."

I must have looked as startled as I felt, because she smiled for the first time. An enchanting smile. *Lucky Victor*, I thought.

"I know it sounds funny," she said, "but the way they say, it could work, only I think the person would maybe kind of have to want to be murdered. Then there's a plastic bag all sealed up in another plastic bag, and it's got 'Don't touch' all over it, so I left it alone. And there's some pictures of a cruddy kitchen counter. That's all."

"Nothing else?"

"No."

I thought it over while I finished my iced tea. I couldn't see offhand what connection the things she had described could have with the man's getting shot in his car three months later. "Hang on to them awhile," I suggested.

"No!" She looked a little frightened. "You take them. Then you can give them to the cops if they need them." She was fum-

[ 68 ]

bling in her purse as she spoke, and she pulled out a fat nine-by-twelve envelope and handed it across the table. "It's all in there, just like he left it."

I looked at the envelope. In the upper left-hand corner someone had printed "Evidence" in tidy block letters. "Did you write that?" I asked.

"No. Victor did."

"How can I get hold of you if I need you?" I asked.

She'd already thought that one out. "Put an ad in the personals column of the *Star*. All you have to say is 'Linda.' Then I'll call you at work."

"Just your name? No message?"

"That's right." She sounded more confident than she had at any time since I'd met her. I wondered whether her name was really Linda and decided it probably wasn't. "I'll be watching for it," she assured me. "And I'll get a friend of mine to watch too, so I won't miss it." She zipped her purse and stood up.

Not until she was already out of the restaurant did I realize that sweet, oh-so-innocent little Linda had stuck me with the check. Well, to be charitable, maybe she forgot.

I tucked my ten-dollar envelope under my arm and set out for home. Karen shouldn't be too upset, I thought, glancing at my watch. I'd be home well before seven, for sure.

The air in 50th Street was thick, as if the young locust trees planted along the brick sidewalk were pressing down against the waves of heat that rose from the pavement. I could actually feel a brief hot draft up my pants leg with each step. The temperature had probably hit close to a hundred that afternoon.

As I turned north on France, I could see the jetliners angling out of the sky ahead of me, air-conditioned airplanes on their way to the air-conditioned airport. So there was hope of more rain, and the temporary relief from the heat it would bring. I tried not to think of the mosquitoes that would follow as the night the day. The loon is the Minnesota state bird, but local T-shirts give that honor to the mosquito, and that's no joke.

It could have been a pleasant walk, if I hadn't felt so guilty. Once you leave 50th Street, there's a continuous residential area between downtown Edina and Lake Harriet, which is in Minneapolis. The residents of the area were taking advantage of the light evening to cut their lawns, and the summer odor of mown grass hung in the air, mixed with the fumes of the mowers. I passed a guy on roller skates, dressed in nothing but ragged cut-offs and a full, curly red beard, pushing a stroller in which a fat-faced baby with flames for hair sat solemnly watching the world roll by. A summer baby must be a wonderful toy, I thought. I'd soon find out. Crossing my fingers for luck, I smiled at the prospect of pushing my own kid around Lake Harriet.

No wild Rabbits this evening. I got to my house without incident, said a quick hello to Celia Dixon, weeding her perennial border next to my driveway, and went around to the back door on the off chance that Karen had left it open in the heat.

She hadn't. I used my key and went into the kitchen, expecting to see her getting dinner ready, but the room was empty.

"Karen?" I called. "I'm home."

No answer. The house was no cooler than the outdoors, the air just as humid. She'd be out talking to one of the neighbors, I decided. Before I went out to look for her, I might as well stash the envelope.

Somewhere Karen wouldn't find it.

After a moment's thought, I went into the family room and slipped the envelope into the box that held *Tosca*. It fit, with a little squashing, into the space that had been meant for the libretto I lost two weeks after I had bought the records, and if Karen ever willingly listened to opera, it was news to me.

I went out the front door, leaving it open. "Seen Karen?" I asked Celia Dixon.

"Gee, no." She pushed her sunhat back. It tumbled off her head, and I retrieved it for her. "Thanks. No, J. J., I haven't seen her at all, not since I got home."

I looked up and down the block. No Karen. I went back into the house.

Where could she be? Sometime during the day she had cut a sheaf of Siberian iris and arranged them in the big green vase on the mantel that had held lilacs two or three weeks before. Her gardening gloves and the shears were on the kitchen table, and the trimmed ends of the flower stalks lay in the sink. Not like Karen, to leave the stems in the sink and not carry them out to the compost pile; not like Karen, to drop the gloves and shears on the table when they had homes in the shoebag on the back of the cellar door. Little prickles of fear ran up my spine.

I dialed the old lady who lives on the other side of us from the Dixons and asked if she'd seen Karen.

"No, I haven't," she said. "She'd have called one of us if the baby decided to come early, wouldn't she?"

"Of course," I said. She'd call, if her husband wasn't buying a girl an uneaten sandwich in a restaurant. "She'll show up pretty soon, I guess."

The instant I hung up on Mrs. Eskew I dialed Methodist Hospital. No, Karen had not been admitted. I called her obstetrician, got the answering service, and was told that she hadn't called since the service took over the phone at five. More than two hours.

"Joe, what on earth are you doing?"

I hung up. Karen leaned against the door frame of the family room. She pushed a wisp of damp hair off her face with a slow hand.

"I couldn't find you," I said. "I got worried."

"I was in the bedroom asleep." She walked unsteadily into the room and plumped down on the edge of the couch. "You can't have looked very hard."

"Are you all right?" I asked. "You look funny."

She put her hands on her swollen belly and stared out the window. "I guess I'm okay," she said. "I feel a little wobbly."

"Should I call the doctor?"

"No," she said. "Maybe. Yes."

So I called the answering service back and we sat down to wait for the doctor to call us. Two tears moved slowly down Karen's sweaty face. "Joe," she said. "I can't remember feeling the baby move all afternoon."

I patted her hand, too scared to do more.

# IX

Maybe ten minutes later, the telephone rang. "I'll get it," Karen said, clumsily unwinding her feet from her tucked-up position on the couch. "I can talk to him better."

I was leaning against the counter in the kitchen, eating some of the potato salad Karen had made that afternoon and trying to persuade her to have something more than the glass of mineral water she had poured for herself. She hauled herself to her feet and got the phone on about the fourth ring. "Hello?" she said.

A long silence. "I beg your pardon?" Her face flushed and she banged the phone onto the hook. "I'm supposed to ask you where you ate supper," she said, turning to face me. "And who the pretty girl is."

"Oh, jeez."

"Well?"

The doorbell chose that precise moment to ring. "It wasn't anything serious, Karen," I said. "I'll tell you all about it in a minute. Go sit down." I put the plate down on the counter next to the stove and went through the living room to answer the door.

Mack was standing on the porch, in uniform. "I thought Minneapolis was somebody else's turf," I said.

"It is. Get in the car."

The car at the curb was only Mack's old Honda. "Mack, I can't go anywhere. Karen's sick."

"Get in the car, dammit!" He waved his hat at the car and set his lower lip in a tight line.

I didn't move.

"Look, I told the sergeant I was gonna deliver you to sign that statement, and I'm not leaving without you."

"I guess you're stuck, then." Behind me, the telephone rang once. "Come in for a minute," I said.

"...Feeling much better," I heard Karen say. "Yes, I guess I did. Oh, is that it?"

"She's feeling better," Mack said. "So get in the car. I'm on duty in twenty minutes."

"Hang on two seconds, can't you?"

Karen came into the living room. "Hi, Mack," she said. She turned to me. "He says it's the heat—I let myself get dehydrated or something. I'm supposed to keep my fluid intake up, fruit juice and stuff."

"What about the baby?"

"He says it's not unusual for them to be pretty still for a few hours, late in pregnancy. He says maybe it will come early. Call him again if it doesn't move soon."

"Glad you're okay," Mack said. To me: "She can drink fruit juice without you. Get in the car."

"Mack wants me to go sign that statement," I told Karen. "From last weekend."

"Right now?"

"Right now," Mack said. "I'd arrest him if he'd get in the car so I can get him over the city line."

Karen looked out the open front door at the Honda. "I wish he didn't have to go," she said. "As long as it's been this long, couldn't it wait a little longer? I'm not feeling quite right yet."

"Tell you what," Mack said. "You come too. I'll drop you off at my house. Mickey's sleeping over at a friend's, and Joy will be glad of the company."

"Well…" Karen sounded unenthusiastic. "Okay. But first let me talk to Joe for a second, will you? Alone?"

"As long as he doesn't go sneaking over the back fence," Mack said.

"We haven't got a back fence," she said. She took my arm and drew me backward into the house, and Mack clattered down the steps.

Karen turned to me. "Where did you eat supper, and who was the girl?"

"I didn't really eat supper. I just had a sandwich and a glass of iced tea. The girl said her name is Linda, no last name, and for all I know it is. She was Victor Amant's 'special friend,' as she puts it."

[ 73 ]

"Amant's the guy who got killed."

I nodded.

"What did she want?"

"Nothing I could make any sense of. Let's go, honey, Mack will be late."

"They won't care, if he brings you." She went over to the mantel and adjusted one of the irises in the green vase. "I wish you wouldn't keep getting mixed up in this, Joe."

"It doesn't leave me alone."

"You could leave *it* alone," she said.

"It was your idea in the first place," I was churlish enough to point out.

"That was before I knew what it was," she said. "I've changed my mind, believe me." She sighed and looked into the mirror behind the irises as if it weren't there. "Let me get my stuff," she said, turning, and went out to the kitchen. I heard the refrigerator open and close, and Karen rinse something in the sink. In a minute or two she returned with her purse. "I wish I could just go back to sleep," she said.

"Why don't you?"

"I don't know. I'll feel better with some company too, I guess." She looked around the living room, flipped on the timed light we leave going to discourage burglars, backtracked to turn off the kitchen light, and came out onto the porch. She must be feeling better, I thought, watching her move.

She grinned at me. "It just kicked," she said.

I bounded down the steps in great relief, although the weather felt more thundery than ever and the jets were still on the western flight path. A huge three-quarter moon had risen above the treetops in the east.

"Feels like rain," Karen said, looking up at the so-far-cloudless sky. "Oh, I wish it would cool off!"

I, too, had the feeling that things might be getting a little too hot for comfort. But that was something else again.

"Grave robbing is a crime, Forrester," Chelon said. "Where'd you dig this one up?"

[74]

"At his house," Mack said. "He wants to get this cleared up just as much as you do, right, J. J.?"

I nodded nervously at Chelon, whose lower lip was lapped over his upper lip. Just thoughtful, maybe, but it made him look disconcertingly like a bulldog. Then he blinked, and the turtle reasserted itself. "We'll go back to my office," he said.

"Sure." I hated the way the word came out: Anything to please you, sir!

"It won't take long," Mack assured me, without taking his big paw off my elbow. "All you have to do is read the thing over and sign it."

I gave my arm a shake, and Mack tightened his grip. "Jeez, Mack, I'm not running away," I protested.

"Sorry. Habit," he said, and dropped his hand. He followed me, and I followed Chelon. I resolved never again to complain about my cramped working quarters. I could end up like Chelon —and would, if anybody ever told my company that people could work in such small spaces.

Chelon sat down at a gray steel desk and looked at me. "Something else has just come up," he said.

Mack slipped sideways around the desk and stood behind Chelon, against the window. He needn't have bothered: adequate precautions against unauthorized exit had already been taken.

"We've had an anonymous tip," Chelon said. "If we search your house, we'll find some evidence tying you to Victor Amant. What do you have to say to that?"

I gaped at him.

Chelon looked down at his desk. "Look for a brown envelope marked 'Evidence,' it says here."

"Holy…!" Words failed. I took a deep breath. "Let me guess. Was it a young woman who called? Sometime past six this evening?"

Chelon blinked twice, but he wasn't about to say yes in so many words. "Why do you ask?"

"Some girl named Linda—at least, she said that was her name —called me at work today. Four times, but I only talked to her

[ 75 ]

twice. First she said she wanted to meet me for lunch, but when I told her my car was in the shop, she decided against it. Then she called back this afternoon and said she wanted to meet me for coffee or a sandwich after work. She said she was Victor Amant's 'special friend' and she wanted to talk to me. So I said okay, and I got my office mate to drive me over there—"

"Over where?" asked Chelon.

I named the restaurant.

"What happened to your car?"

Mack, behind Chelon, had his lips thrust forward in a big, silent *no.*

"I, ah, smacked it into somebody in the parking lot at work."

"Any injuries?"

"No. Just a lot of crumpled sheet metal."

Chelon was taking notes. "That all?" he asked. "No police investigation?"

Mack shook his head furiously.

"Er, no." Behind Chelon, Mack moved his hands out and down, palms toward the floor. Safe.

"Okay. Go on about this girl."

"She said she needed advice. She said Victor Amant's car had been tampered with last spring, and he'd given her this envelope to hold. She didn't know what to do with it. So she—"

"Amant's car had been tampered with?" Chelon said. "Did she say how?"

The index and middle fingers of Mack's right hand crept along his horizontal left forearm, like a man walking on thin ice. "Somebody screwed around with the brake line," I said.

"Ah. Okay."

"Anyhow, she was going to leave it up to me to decide if the police would want this envelope."

"So where is it?"

"At my house, like she said."

Chelon let that pass. "What's in it?"

"I haven't had a chance to look. She said there was a Xerox of part of some book about how to murder people." Here Chelon grinned and Mack rolled his eyes toward heaven. "There was a

[ 76 ]

plastic bag," I went on, "sealed up in another plastic bag—it was labeled 'Don't touch,' so she didn't, she said—and a picture of a kitchen."

"Okay, we'll catch that later. Now I want you to sign this." Chelon found a folder in a stack on the desk and gave it to me.

I read, in oddly stilted language, an account of the events of the preceding Friday night and Saturday morning. It all seemed accurate enough, so I signed each page at the bottom, slowly shaking my head.

"What's the matter?" Chelon asked.

"You know," I remarked, "I can't remember one damned thing about that movie I saw Friday."

Chelon sat up straighter. Mack pantomimed a faint.

"It'll come to me, I guess," I said. Not good enough: the sergeant was writing himself a note.

"What did this Linda look like?" he asked.

I told him: shoulder length, dark, curly hair, held back from her face with brown plastic combs, big hazel eyes with long dark lashes, my varying estimates of her age, her petite figure, what she'd been wearing.

"In Edina," Chelon said. "What a drag." He sat looking at his notes for a moment, then swiveled and looked up at Mack. "Forrester, take this guy back to his house and get me that envelope."

"He lives in Minneapolis, and we don't have a warrant," Mack pointed out.

I thought Chelon might explode. "Forget that," I said. "You can have the damn envelope, and welcome. Just as long as I don't have to bring it by bus."

"Now you're making sense," said Chelon. As if I hadn't before.

Mack and I went back out into the evening. The moon was higher, riding on a cushion of haze that turned its lower edge a dull orange; heat climbed out of the pavement with malice aforethought. "We'll take my car," Mack said. "It's not air-conditioned, but it's not so conspicuous, either. Save spraining your neighbors' eyeballs."

"And besides, I don't live in St. Louis Park."

"So?" He slid into the driver's seat while I rounded the back of the car. The passenger-side door drifted open ahead of Mack's hand just as I got to it, and I folded myself into the other front seat.

The lights were with us. Ten minutes later I was unlocking my front door while Mack jittered behind me. "That girl really set you up, you know?" he said. "I sure wish I could figure where she fits in."

"You and me both, old buddy," I said. I flipped on a light in the family room and retrieved the envelope from *Tosca.*

"That Leontyne Price, she's some singer," Mack said. I tried to hand him the envelope. "No, you hang on to it. That way, you can give it straight to Chelon and swear it's the same one."

"I suppose I'll have to sign another statement," I grumped.

"You want him to make something up?"

"You've got a point."

The telephone rang. Mack jerked his head toward it. I went into the kitchen and picked it up.

"Hi, Mr. Jamison? It's Linda. I'm glad I caught you—I've been trying all evening."

"What do you want, Linda?" I asked. Mack dropped the *Tosca* box and hotfooted it for the bedroom. I heard the soft click of the other phone being lifted as she answered.

"You gonna be home for a while?"

"What for?"

"I need to see you again," she said. "I've thought of something else I need advice about."

"Can't you ask over the phone?"

"Uh, no, not really." The juvenile voice sounded strained. "Can I come over? I don't live far."

"Can't you tell me what it's about?" I squinted at the clock. Jeez, almost ten already. "It's pretty late."

"Not on the phone," she insisted. "It's about that envelope. You have still got it, don't you?"

"Sure," I said, strictly honest, "but I'm going out for a little bit. I should be back by eleven."

"Okay." She hung up.

Mack came out of the bedroom. "Doesn't have much to say, does she?"

"You're a breather, Mack. You scared her off."

"What do you want, with this heat?" He wiped the sweat from under his chin with the back of one hand. "That was good, pretending you didn't know she'd informed on you. I wish you'd got more out of her, though."

"I did what I could, dammit."

"Wonder what she wants." He scratched his chest through his shirt and shrugged. "Let's get this over with. You got that envelope?"

"Hang on a sec. I want to start the fan in the bedroom."

"Make it quick, will you?"

I went into the bedroom, raised the window all the way, and started the window fan going. With any luck it would suck a little hot air out of the room before I got back.

"You got that envelope?" Mack asked again, as we walked out the front door. I held it up for him to see and pulled the door shut behind me.

"You oughta get a deadbolt," Mack said. "Those spring locks are practically useless."

"I never had any trouble."

"Dumb luck." We got into his car. "I guess you're gonna need some dumb luck," he added. "Somebody's sure got it in for you. I wouldn't let that Linda in my house, I'll tell you that."

"I'm bigger than she is."

"Yeah. What if she's got a gun? They didn't used to call them equalizers for nothing."

"Okay, so I'll be careful. But I don't think she'll shoot me, not when she's gone to the trouble of calling the cops on me."

Mack jerked the car into gear, and we roared down the hill to Xerxes. "All the same, I don't like it. I can't make any sense out of it, and I don't like things I can't make sense out of."

"Come back with me then."

His eyes slid toward me as he braked for a stop sign. "Not a bad idea. I'll be on duty, but I'll figure something."

Neither of us said any more. I looked for the moon's reflection in Lake Calhoun as we sped along the west shore, but it wasn't there. Finally, I realized that the sky had clouded over. I hoped it would get the rain over with soon.

Five pictures spilled out of the envelope, not one. A view of a large, neat kitchen. A view of one end of the same kitchen. A birch tree grew close enough to the window to brush the window with its catkins, among which redpolls were feeding. A closeup of a section of counter under the window, showing an oddly roughened surface on which a fuzzy white something rested. Then a harsh portrait of a woman lying in bed, gazing away into space with the covers pulled up half over her face, that gave me shivers. And last, a full view of the bedroom, with the woman lying in bed in the same position.

Chelon tossed the closeup of the woman across his desk. "You know her?"

"No."

"What do you make of it?" His gesture took in all the contents of the envelope.

"Nothing," I said. "I can't put it together."

"If we knew just what we're looking at, I bet we'd have the whole story," Chelon mused.

Mack said, "Maybe it means that the woman was killed the way it says on that paper."

"How would anybody know?"

"What do you want, everything?" Mack picked up the Xeroxed sheet and read it over. The part about carbon dioxide had been underlined, and someone had written "Lala?" in the margin.

"Sounds like a politician's dog," Chelon grumbled. "That underlining was done in the book, right?"

"Or on another Xerox," I said. "Of which this is a copy."

Chelon looked at me as if he had forgotten my existence. "Who asked you?"

He had typed out a statement for me to sign while Mack and I were gone. It needed a couple of minor corrections, which I wrote in and all of us initialed. The phone rang while I was signing all the pages.

"Okay, Jamison, that's all we need you for right now," Chelon said. "Now you might as well get on over to Methodist. Your wife's having a baby."

My mouth went loose and I stared at him. He turned to Mack. "That was your wife. She's at the hospital too." He turned back to me. "Well, don't just sit there, Jamison. There's a pay phone in the lobby; go call yourself a cab."

I dropped the quarter on the floor three times. Finally, Mack, on his way out, picked it up and shoved it into the phone for me, dialed, and handed me the receiver. I had to clear my throat twice before I could order the cab.

Karen looked a lot better than she had earlier that evening, even in the hospital johnny that matched the pattern of one of my pairs of shorts. She was excited and happy. I was excited and scared.

I did all the little things I could do: helped her to the bathroom when the nurse wanted her to go, rubbed her back for the contractions, held her hand, wiped the sweat off her face when the work got hard. And when the baby was finally born, the doctor handed me a pair of scissors, and *I* cut the cord.

At 5:27 on a bright, thunderstorm-cleared morning, I held an incredibly tiny son in my arms and cried with pure happiness. Yes, tears. If you're thinking of laughing at me, try it yourself sometime and see if you don't do the same.

A couple of hours later, after the long-distance calls to the grandparents and aunts and uncles had been made ("J. J.," my older sister said, "I'm really happy for you, but do you have any idea what time it is in San Diego?") and we'd spent some time with our new child, Karen fell asleep. I swiped some cash from her purse and took advantage of the pass I'd been given to have a plate of eggs and bacon and hash browns in the hospital cafeteria. Then I called another cab and went home.

The cab pulled up in front of the house, and the cabbie looked at it without opening the door. "That one?" he said. "Gee, it looks like you had a fire."

I stopped fumbling with my wallet and looked. The corner of the house was blackened and wet. There was a hole in the roof about over the bedroom, and the shrubs Karen had nurtured so carefully were trampled and broken. The grass had been torn up by something dragging over it: hose connections, maybe. I sat in the back of the cab and stared at it.

"Mister? You okay?"

"Yeah, I think so," I said. "I guess so."

"You want me to take you someplace else?"

Where?

"No. I think I better get out and see if one of the neighbors can tell me what happened." I opened my wallet.

"Forget it," the cabbie said. "You had a rough enough night as it is."

*You don't know the half of it*, I thought. "No, take it," I said, holding out a five. "Thanks, but there's no reason you should give me a free ride just because I've got a little trouble."

The guy took the five and started to make change. "You can keep it," I said, and got out.

He rolled down his window. "Hey, you want me to wait? I'll keep it off the meter."

"No, that's okay. Thanks." The cabbie rolled the window back up on his wheezy air conditioning and drove slowly away toward the lake.

I went up the walk and onto the squishy lawn. The glass was gone from the front-bedroom window, whether because the heat of the fire had broken it or because some fireman had taken his ax to it, I didn't know. I looked in.

A blackish room with water on the floor, a half-burned mattress dragged off the bed. Part of the side wall was gone. The daisies on what was left of the wallpaper looked stunned.

I walked around the side of the house and tripped over the cord of the phone that had lived on the bedside table. It didn't look at all damaged, so I picked up the receiver and listened. Dead, of course. No sign of the window fan. The bathroom looked okay from outside; the back bedroom, still half my study and only half converted into a room for little Joey, had water stains on the inside walls but seemed otherwise undisturbed.

"J. J.?"

The little old lady who lived on that side of us had her face pressed to the screen of her dining-room window. All her rose bushes were broken down, I saw, the bright new petals of the first blooms ground into the mud. "I'm sorry, Mrs. Eskew," I said.

"Sorry? Oh, the roses. They'll come back. It's your house I'm worried about. Come in and have some coffee, will you, dear?"

"Thanks," I said. "That sounds like something I need."

[ 82 ]

In her dim, old-fashioned dining room with the cabbage roses on the wallpaper and the peaceful white-painted woodwork, Mrs. Eskew poured coffee into a fine porcelain cup and offered me a dollop of whiskey from a crystal decanter, which I turned down.

"J. J.," she said, when I had had a sip of her mocha-java and set the cup down. "That fire was set."

"Set? I don't understand." I had been thinking of lightning or a short in the 1947 wiring, things of that sort.

Mrs. Eskew leaned forward, all business. "I heard a noise about two o'clock this morning, and I got up and looked out. You know, when you're old you don't sleep so well as you do when you're younger, and the heat was just awful before the storm broke. So I woke up right away, even though it was a very *faint* noise."

She picked up her silver pot and poured more coffee into my cup. "Well, there was a man doing something near your window, the one with the fan in it. I thought he might be trying to break in. I went and got my pistol just in case, and I was going to call out to him, to ask him what he was doing. But before I could, a big flame shot up, and he ran away through your backyard! I was so surprised I didn't even think to shoot him. So I called the fire department instead."

"Thank you," I said. I shivered. It felt as though the temperature in her dining room had dropped ten degrees in the last ten seconds.

"They were here very fast, but the fire had such a good start — I told one of the firemen what I had seen, and he said, yes, they could smell the kerosene! Oh, J. J., if I had only waked up a little sooner!"

"I'm glad you woke up when you did," I said. "The whole house might have gone, otherwise."

She nodded, looking at me over the rims of her glasses. "There's that," she said, not sounding much consoled. "And I am very glad you weren't sleeping in that room. I thought you might be dead! Such a relief to learn the house was empty." She cocked her head at me. "Where is Karen, by the way?"

"Oh! Karen had her baby! We have a son."

Mrs. Eskew dimpled and bustled and called a couple of neighbors and fed me English muffins and homemade crabapple jelly I didn't really want and advised me earnestly not to worry Karen with news of the fire right away.

"I should call my insurance company," I said.

"Oh! Use my telephone. I'm so glad I can help somehow."

"I have to go home and look up the agent's number anyway," I said. "So if my kitchen phone's working, I'll just use that."

"All right. If you say so."

"Thanks for breakfast. And thank you for calling the fire department."

"Oh, any time! Any time at all!"

I didn't point out that I hoped the occasion wouldn't arise too frequently. At her back door, something else occurred to me. "You didn't get a look at the man running away, did you?"

"No. He was tall, that's all I can tell you. And wearing a ski mask. I hope he died of heat exhaustion," she added, pinching her lips together.

I nodded and thanked her some more and went home. I'd have to come back to use her phone after all, I saw: my own telephone line lay in the back yard, disattached from the house. I picked up the end of the cable and saw that it had been neatly severed, the line pinched up across the end of the wires showing that it had been cut. I'd never heard of firemen cutting telephone lines. The electric lines were still in place.

I let myself in the back door, retrieved the insurance policy from the freezer, where we keep it in case of fire, and found the list of numbers I would have to call.

# X

I used Mrs. Eskew's phone to tell Pedersen I had a new son and a partially burned house and wouldn't be in that day. He advised me against further celebration and congratulated me on not having fathered quintuplets, "or the whole house might have gone. And Jamison? I've found the reason for Hudson's expenses. Disappointing, I must say. He is executor for the estate of some relative and has advanced the legal fees. Alas."

"Alas. Look, I've got to go." Pedersen promised to tell the right people I wouldn't be in, and I hung up.

You don't see much of the aftermath of a fire on TV. Just flames shooting up, or bodies carried away. Luckily, this time there were no bodies for the camera crew to floodlight, and I'd arrived hours after the flames were out. I thanked Mrs. Eskew for her phone, borrowed her car, and set to work.

I had to get hold of some cheap plywood to put over the holes in the house. This is called "securing the premises against further damage," and you'd better have a damned good reason for not doing it, or the insurance company gets picky about paying your claim. Check your own policy if you don't believe me.

So I borrowed a roof rack for Mrs. Eskew's Chevy from the Dixons, trucked on over to Fifth Avenue and picked up some water-damaged C-D plywood from the lumberyard there, and nailed it up. While I was trying to wrestle a sheet of the stuff onto the roof, one of the guys the insurance agent had put me on to came by to give me an estimate on the damage. The plywood slid off the roof and decapitated half a row of Karen's irises.

The guy, another big blond, considered my house, considered the slump in the building industry, and suggested putting on a second story while I was at it. I told him I'd be happy to get shingles on the roof. He suggested going with cedar. I decided to wait for another bid.

And so on, and so on. Around three, I found time for a quick lunch at the Tastee Treat on 44th, and called Mack from a near-by pay phone.

"What do you mean, you got burned out?" he asked. "What kind of kid did you have?"

"A boy." I waited impatiently through his congratulations. "Now can I tell you about the house?"

"I wish I'd never called you about that UFO," Mack complained. "I'm never gonna catch up on my sleep at this rate."

"You and me both, Mack."

"Where are you now?"

"On 44th, near the Red Owl." It's a supermarket.

"Hang on. I'll come get you."

I went into the florist on the corner while I waited, and ordered a bouquet of white carnations to be sent to Karen. Then I went back to the pay phone and put in a call to the hospital, only to have her roommate tell me she was sleeping. I said to tell her I'd be in to see her a little later, and hung up just as Mack's little blue car pulled up to the curb.

"Let's go look at your house," he said.

"Gonna play detective?"

Mack was in a good mood; he laughed. "Yeah, you and me, we're the Hardy Boys."

"I already did that," I said. "So did the insurance adjuster and the fire department."

"The more, the merrier." He grinned. "Chelon will have a kitten."

"Can I watch?"

"You don't want to, believe me." He pulled up in front of my house, which stared back at us with its one blind eye where the bedroom window used to be.

"I see you got the bandages on," Mack said. "Why didn't you call before? I could have given you a hand." He was out of the car, walking across the lawn and around the side of the house. He kicked at the pile of ashes under what used to be the side bedroom window. "Looks like straw."

"Whole bale of the stuff. Karen had it in the garage, left over from mulching the strawberries last fall."

He sniffed. "Kerosene?"

"That's what they tell me."

He put his hands on his hips and looked down at the pile of ashes. "I s'pose you've got one of those heaters."

"No. He brought his own fuel."

Mack walked around the back corner of the house and gazed up at the cut end of the telephone wire that was tapping against the house in the slight breeze. "I wonder how come he didn't just cut it where it goes into the house, instead of reaching way up like that?"

"Search me," I said. "My investigations are usually on a higher level."

Mack gave me a disgusted glance. "I hope you don't expect me to laugh at that."

I shrugged. "Suit yourself."

Mack gave the free end of the telephone line a kick and continued his circuit of the house. "You were supposed to be in there, you know. When it caught."

I felt a little chill go down my back. "What do you mean, in there?"

"In the house, dummo. What do you think all that exercise was last night? That girl calling?"

"Linda?"

"Whatever. She was setting you up. I bet she never showed up here at eleven. I bet she was miles away, getting herself seen in some bar."

I stuck my hands in my pockets and followed him down the driveway, shaking my head. Staying up all night does nothing for the little gray cells. A slick of drying mud covered the end of the driveway, where the water had sluiced off the lawn. Mack teetered along the brick edge of Celia Dixon's flowerbed to avoid dirtying his shoes.

"I can't figure it," I said. "Why call the cops, then? To get the envelope out before the house burned down? And what did she have against me in the first place?"

"How the hell should I know? I'm not up on how you treat your dinner dates. Maybe she didn't like her soup."

"She didn't have soup."

"Your guess is as good as mine, then."

I slammed the door of the little car and fastened the shoulder belt as Mack took off.

"Where are we going now?" I asked as he gunned across Xerxes Avenue.

"Over to Methodist. I figured you might want to visit your wife and child. Besides, I got to get a nap. It's Friday, dammit."

I promised to give him my phone number as soon as I had one, and he let me out in front of the big glass doors of the hospital. I pushed through them for the fourth time that week.

In the end, I told Karen that we'd had a fire but not how it started.

"Where are we going to take Joey when it's time for us to go home?" she asked.

"I'm not sure yet," I told her. "The insurance agent says the Red Cross might help me find a temporary apartment, but I haven't had time to ask. If things go quickly enough, maybe we can use part of the house while they finish fixing it. I don't know."

"At least it's not winter," she sighed. And it wasn't: clouds, big, white thunderclouds, were peeking over the horizon again when I left the hospital. I took a cab home to pick up some clothes. Not so generous with the tip this time. The cash I'd swiped from Karen at the hospital was running low. I got a room in a motel on Excelsior Boulevard, picked up some Kentucky Fried Chicken for supper, and called Joy Forrester to let Mack know where I was. Then, at her suggestion, I called the phone company and arranged for a message to go on my own phone, telling callers to call me at the motel.

It wasn't twenty minutes later that a heavy fist was applied to the door of my room.

The fist belonged to Mack Forrester. "I got a nasty job for you, J. J.," he said soberly. "We just found a body that fits the description of that girl who gave you the envelope. We need an ID."

I hung on to the door frame. "Mack, I don't know how much more I can take," I said. "Can't you find me a nice, mysterious light in the sky at the declination of Venus, or a little green man or two? Tomorrow?"

Mack's big chest expanded. His blond moustache fluttered

as he exhaled. "Sorry. We have to take what we get in this business. You know that."

"Yeah. Well, let me get my shoes on."

Mack waited while I fished my joggers out of the shag rug and put them on. I chunked the fried-chicken package into the wastebasket and followed him out.

"Got your key?"

"Uh-huh." Mack reached behind me and slammed the door.

I got in the back of the squad car, and Mack pulled out onto Excelsior, headed west. His partner, a black guy neither of them bothered to introduce, sat in the front seat without speaking and stared out the passenger-side window. "Where are we going?" I asked.

"Out 12 a ways." Mack glanced into the rearview mirror as he spoke. The radio crackled, something incomprehensible. Neither cop seemed to pay the slightest attention. Mack swung down the ramp to Highway 100, slipped quietly into the stream of home-going traffic, and headed north. To my left, the line of thunderheads shouldered above the horizon, as they had almost every day for the past ten, already turning from the white mountains of an hour ago to gray. June. Mosquito heaven. With my luck, a tornado would blow my house away the minute it was fixed. It wasn't so long ago one had passed two blocks away.

Another squad car and an ambulance were pulled up at the south side of Highway 12, two or three miles west of where it crosses 100. Not much activity, other than the swing of the red lights on the vehicles. A group of men, some of them in police blue, stood around the mouth of a culvert that passed under an access road, slapping at their bare arms, and one uniformed officer stood at the edge of the highway, motioning cars past. Mack picked up his microphone, keyed it, and muttered something I couldn't hear.

"Here?" I asked.

Mack's partner turned his head and nodded a fraction, proving he wasn't the plastic figure I had begun to suspect he might be.

Mack went past the spot—12 is a divided highway—and made a U-turn through one of the graveled places provided for such purposes. The car heaved itself onto the pavement going the other way, and we coasted up to the other police vehicles.

One of the men I recognized: Chelon. He gave me an unreadable glance and motioned to Mack. The partner got out and let me out of the back of the car. I went reluctantly toward the group.

Chelon took my arm. "I want you to take a look at this girl and see if you know her, Jamison," he said. A few drops of rain spattered into the dust as he began to lead me down the bank. The dirt was wetter there. "Good Christ, won't it ever stop raining?" the sergeant groused.

She'd been there awhile. Even somebody as untutored as me could see that. Last night's brief shower had washed some sand, the soft pale sand that turns up from place to place in this area, up against her body and then had carved it out again in a series of curves. The hazel eyes were open but not very hazel, already sinking into the skull and being attended to by ants. I retched.

"Don't puke on her!" Chelon gave an alarmed tug on my arm. "You know her?"

I couldn't stop looking. The combs had been disarranged, but they still held her hair. "It's that girl we were talking about last night," I said. "Linda. She's still wearing the same shirt." She'd changed the suit for white shorts, though, and sandals. I wished, inanely, that I could at least push the combs back in place in the tangled hair. Then I saw that the hair wasn't just out of place; the whole skull was misshapen, and the hair was matted with something dark behind the left ear. Blood, probably. I retched again.

Chelon took me by my shoulders and turned me around. "Okay," he said. "What would you say if I told you her name was really Eileen?"

"So she lied. I thought she probably had." The colonel's chicken signaled a strong desire to return to Kentucky. I swallowed, hard.

"Okay," Chelon said to Mack. "Take him in and have him sign a statement."

Mack took me by the elbow and helped me stumble back up the embankment to the car. Behind me, I heard Chelon say, "Okay, let's have the bag."

*What bag?* I wondered. A spritz of rain hit the squad car as Mack opened the door. I tumbled in and leaned my head against the seat.

"Your stomach okay?" Mack asked. "Let me know in time, so I can stop, check?"

"Check," I said. Mack shut the door on me, and I leaned forward and hung my head between my knees. The two front doors slammed, and the car gritted its way onto the highway and shifted up to speed.

A couple of minutes later, I picked up my head and found the unidentified black policeman staring at me. I tried a smile, which didn't come out very well, and he presented me with about half of one of his own and turned his head back to look out the windshield. The wipers were going double speed.

Mack glanced at me in the rearview mirror. "Feeling any better?"

"A little."

He slowed for the light at Vernon. A clap of thunder shook the car. All three of us jumped.

"You are one lucky guy, you know that, J. J.?" Mack said.

"I don't feel all that lucky."

"Lucky," Mack repeated. "You had a witness to that call the girl made last night, and you can account for every minute between then and eight o'clock this morning."

"I can?" I said, without much interest.

"That cabbie who took you home remembered you, because of the fire, the nurses on the ward remembered when you arrived and left—"

"Okay, okay."

"And since it quit raining around seven, you're covered."

The black policeman shifted a little in his seat, radiating disapproval.

"That's marvelous," I said. I felt as if my life had been dirtied somehow. I was not going to connect this business with the rest of my life, my real life. This was only a dream, and it would go away, just as soon as I figured out how to wake up.

But the dream continued, while Mack typed out a brief statement of identification with four lickety-split fingers, pondering aloud the senselessness of the whole business. "We'll get the

[ 91 ]

ballistics back, and five will get you twenty it will turn out the same .22 shot this lady as shot your friend Amant," he said. "But I'm damned if I can tell you why."

"Not my friend," I said mechanically.

"Whatever you want to call him, then." Mack surveyed his typing critically. "That's it. Sign here."

I skimmed the four sentences and signed. "This is getting to be a habit," I said.

"Yeah, and who would have thought it when we were playing Little League together?" Mack stood up. "You can go home now."

"Back to the motel, you mean." I stayed in my chair, suddenly too fatigued even to think about standing up, and rubbed my face. "And on the bus. I don't even have cab fare with me."

"Ah, hell, I can lend you five bucks, even on a cop's pay," he said. "Hold on, I have to get it from my locker."

I waited while he disappeared. The black cop sat like the plastic figure I had wondered about, utterly calm and silent. I guessed he had nothing to say, but the effect was to make me feel like babbling about the weather. *He must be a good man in an interrogation,* I thought. Could probably get a full confession to anything without ever opening his mouth.

Mack came back and held out a five and a quarter for the phone. Suddenly I remembered something else.

"Mack, here's another one for you," I said. "That girl gave me a way to get in touch with her."

The black cop shifted beside me. Mack raised his eyebrows.

"She said, put an ad in the *Star* and she'd call me at work. She said she'd watch for it, get a friend to watch for it too. So why would she set me up for that fire?"

"You tell me," Mack said. "Look, I got work to do."

I got the money in the slot myself this time and called a cab. Then I followed Mack and the other cop out of the building. They made a dash through the rain to their car, and I stayed in the doorway, waiting for the cab. It took its own sweet time coming.

The phone was ringing again when I had paid off the cab and put my key in the lock. I collapsed on the purple bedspread that some maniac decorator had chosen for the motel and picked the receiver up.

"This is Prunella Watson," said the dry old voice I'd come to know so well since joining CATCH three years before. "I have a report of a multiple sighting near Mud Butte, South Dakota. I wish you'd take a look."

"Prue, I just can't," I said. "My wife just had a baby, my car's in the repair shop, I had a fire in my house last night, and I've managed to get myself mixed up in the fringes of a murder investigation."

"You know what they say—if you want something done, ask a busy man," she said cheerily.

"Yeah, well, this man is half-dead," I replied. "Call what's-his-face in Pierre."

"He's in Hawaii for two weeks," she said bleakly. "Have you got another name?"

"Sorry, Prue. I'm at a motel and my records are at home."

"Not burnt, I hope!"

"Not burnt," I assured her. We chatted a few minutes longer; she wheedled, I held firm. She congratulated me on the birth of my son and gloomily decided to ask the Idaho-Montana-Wyoming man to take the sighting. I hung up and wondered if going to bed really required getting out of my clothes. I had just decided it didn't, when the phone rang.

"J. J., it's Anne Streich," said the voice. "I've been trying to get you all afternoon."

"I'm sorry," I said. "I've been pretty busy." The ceiling wavered momentarily as I opened my eyes.

"I've got the name of the boy who was talking to David in Shakey's last week," she said. "You wanted to ask him some questions?"

"Oh. Yes." I couldn't imagine what questions I could possibly have wanted to ask, right off the bat.

"He's eager to talk to you, too," Anne said. "And he says he's free this evening. Could you go to his house?"

"Anne, I don't have a car." Using her first name made my mind fizz. "I smacked mine up, and it's being fixed."

"Oh, dear. Harry's at a meeting in Bloomington, and I lent

mine to my brother-in-law. Otherwise, I'd— I have an idea. Can you get yourself over here? I could call Bob and ask him to come over too. Then I could hear what he has to say."

"I could," I said. *No, you couldn't,* my spine objected. *I'm staying right here on this bed.* "But it's likely to take me a while. I'd be walking." *So much for you, spine!*

"It's not far from your house to mine."

"I'm not at my house. I'm at a motel. We had a fire last night."

"Oh, how awful! And your wife's pregnant! Is she all right?"

"She's fine. She's not pregnant any more, though. She had a little boy early this morning." I felt uncomfortable making the announcement: a week ago, Anne Streich had still had a son.

Stern stuff, that woman. "Why, how wonderful!" she exclaimed. I let her gush a while, shaved off two days' worth of beard, took a quick shower, and put on some fresh clothes.

Then I grabbed my umbrella and set out, telling my legs all they had to do was keep putting my feet in front of me, left, right, left, right...just like that.

# XI

Bob Evans had already arrived by the time I had negotiated the mile and a half of dripping dark that separated the motel from the Streichs' big house. It was obvious from his manner that Anne had known all along who he was and had just wanted to check with him before giving me his name. He was a freckle-faced kid a little younger than Dave, with a likable grin. His chin-length, straggly hair and the jeans with the hole in the knee didn't exactly project an aura of wealth, but he fit into the Streichs' polished house in some subtle way I couldn't quite define.

The boy acknowledged Anne Streich's introduction with a well-bred handshake and pleased-to-meet-you. "Anne says you wanted to talk to me about Dave," he said. "What did you want to know?"

My head was buzzing tired. "I'm not quite sure," I said. "Mostly, I think, I just want you to tell me what happened last Friday night."

He glanced at his friend's mother a little doubtfully. She was sitting with her hands folded calmly in her lap, her legs crossed loosely at the ankles, and she gave him an encouraging nod. "Well," he said, "I met Dave around eight-thirty, so we could get everything ready."

"Ready?" Anne frowned.

"For the UFO."

"So it was Dave," she sighed, and seemed to sink into the down pillows of the pale green silk couch.

"I thought you knew?"

She tilted her head toward me. "Mr. Jamison told me, but I hoped he was wrong. After the last one..."

"But this couldn't have started any fires," Bob said. "Anyway, I was helping him because this was a pretty complicated operation. It was only to play a joke on somebody. Dave wouldn't have done it if he had thought it could really hurt anything."

"No, I guess not." Anne sighed. "I hope not." We dropped into silence, Anne still relaxed against the couch, Bob Evans starting to twist his hands together. She looked at me. "Would you like something? Coffee?"

Startled, I nodded.

"Let's go into the kitchen, then," she said. "I'm more comfortable there."

We trooped through an elegant formal dining room in which two cabinets built into the corners of the room shone soft lights onto a collection of china displayed on glass shelves, and around a darkly gleaming table with eight slender chairs pushed up to its edge. Antiques, probably, that Karen would have given her right arm to own. In the kitchen, that trusty servant Mr. Coffee had already prepared a pot of aromatic liquid. Anne reached into a cabinet above the coffeemaker and took down three stoneware mugs, into which she poured coffee with a look of great concentration.

"Cream, anyone? Sugar?"

Both Bob and I shook our heads, and she set a cup in front of each of us. "Cookies," she muttered, turning back to the cabinets with a confused air.

"That's okay," I said. "Just the coffee is fine."

"Bob?" Her voice sounded stronger. She'd decided to accept Dave's part in the hoax, I thought.

"No, thanks."

She already had a box in her hand. She put a few cookies on a plate despite our refusal and set the plate exactly in the center of the round table. I sipped at my coffee. It was hot and strong, and I hoped it would keep me awake, if not alert.

"I don't know if you figured out the contraption we made," Bob said to me.

"Sort of."

"It was pretty neat," Bob said, his voice vivid with pride. "We cut some acrylic into real thin strips and used a hair dryer to heat it so we could bend it into a frame—"

"So that's where my hair dryer went," Anne murmured.

"—glued it together with epoxy. That made the frame transparent, see, so it wouldn't show so much when we put the light

[96]

inside. Then we covered the frame with tissue paper and varnished the whole job with a couple of coats of polyurethane, to keep it from dissolving on us, since the guy Dave was working for said rain or shine."

Anne's head snapped up. "He was working for someone?"

Bob nodded.

"You don't know who?" I asked.

He shook his head. "Sorry. Anyway, we lit the inside with one of those fluorescent camp lanterns. It wasn't perfect, but from a few feet away in the dark, it looked pretty spooky. Then Dave had the idea to put the green and white lights flashing on the top. That made things a little more complicated, because we needed a power source. So we wired some auto batteries together for that, but we lost them when one of the canoes went over."

"Oh?"

"Yeah." Bob looked disgusted. "We dunked the whole job, just as we were about to go under the bridge. We had a lot of trouble trying to clean up, let me tell you, what with the rain and the creek being high from all the wet weather we've had."

Bob sighed. "Then the canoe with the batteries in it capsized under the bridge, and the batteries fell into the creek. We couldn't do anything about it in the dark. The saucer broke up, too, and all we could find was the lantern. Dave was really mad. He'd promised this guy there wouldn't be any 'debris,' he called it."

I looked under the table. Bob was wearing a pair of waffle-tread joggers. "Those the shoes you were wearing?" I asked.

"Yeah. How'd you know?"

"You left tracks."

"Oh, yeah. All that mud." Bob looked down at his cup and circled it with his hands. "I was supposed to meet Dave the next morning good and early and get everything out of the creek, but I called by here and Anne"—he nodded at her; she too, stared into her mug—"told me about the accident. So I—I kind of couldn't. I went home. And I thought, well, I'll go back and get the stuff tomorrow. Only I still haven't got around to it. Might as well stay there, now, I guess."

"Somebody should clean it up," Anne said. "Where did you boys change your clothes?"

It takes a mother to think of that kind of thing. "In the car," Bob said. Anne shook her head parentally.

"How big was this saucer?" I asked.

"Oh, five feet across. See, that's why we had to take a chance on somebody seeing us set it up in daylight. But the weather looked so cruddy, we figured nobody would be paddling down the creek on a Friday night...." Bob shook his head slowly. "And nobody did. We got the thing up and balanced on these struts we had made, with the canoes lashed together. Dave wanted it to be a real neat job, even though this guy was just having it done to make somebody in the hospital laugh." Bob frowned. "I never dreamed he'd pay as much as he did. I just went along for the fun of it."

"How much did he pay?" Anne asked.

"I don't know altogether, but Dave gave me five hundred bucks."

"That's twelve hundred," I said, proud that I could still do simple arithmetic, tired as I was.

Bob whistled.

"For a joke?" Anne said.

"How did you get paid?"

"Well, the guy said he was going to have somebody be a look-out, to make sure the saucer went on schedule, see? Then he was going to meet Dave at Shakey's and pay him. So we were sitting there eating pizza, when all the sudden Dave said, 'I just saw him go by,' and got up and ran out. And a minute later he came back and handed me five hundred-dollar bills and said, 'There's yours.'"

"What did you think of that?"

"Well, what do you think?" Bob's gray eyes opened wide. "I was pretty shocked, but I just tried to act cool, you know? It seemed like a hell of a lot of money for a joke, like you say."

"What if it wasn't a joke?"

The freckled face only looked puzzled. "What do you mean? What could it be? It didn't *do* anything."

"Would you say it was an attention getter?"

Bob grinned. "I hope so."

[ 98 ]

"So somebody seeing it go by would notice that, and not something going on somewhere else in the parking lot?"

"Like what?"

"Like a man getting shot to death."

Anne's hands jerked, and the boy's face paled so that the freckles seemed to get darker. "Jesus," he breathed. "And Dave was in on that?"

"No!" Anne said. "Not Dave. Not possible."

I looked down at the polished wood of the kitchen table and thought briefly of the fake wood grain of my own. "I don't think Dave knew what was going on. He may have been just as surprised at the money as Bob and trying to stay laid back himself. Or if he needed money and knew the person who wanted the joke played, he may just have decided he didn't want to know why it was worth so much."

"Dave didn't run around with murderers," Anne said.

The three of us sat in uncomfortable silence for several minutes. The rain had begun again, tapping against the diamond-paned kitchen windows with their row of potted herbs lined up on the dark wood sill. I saw a flash of lightning, muted to a flare of light by the big old trees around the house.

Bob made a funny noise and reached out for a cookie. Anne's eyes flicked toward the cookie, on its way to Bob's mouth. "I guess it is possible," she said. "You don't know what people are capable of, even when you've had over forty years' experience. And Dave was trying to pay his father back for the damage done in that fire, the last time he got into this kind of thing. That much money must have looked very tempting."

Neither Bob nor I found anything to say to that. I took another swig of coffee. Thunder sounded, half a mile away. Suddenly Anne brought her fist down on the table with such force that the cups jumped. "And I was *there!*" she said through her teeth. "I was right next door, drinking a vodka martini and eating steak and scallops while that…that *monster* was paying off my son…." Her eyes met mine. "And fixing his car to kill him," she added in a wondering voice.

Bob quietly put his cookie down and turned to me. "The car was fixed?" he asked, voice breaking.

I nodded.

[ 99 ]

"Oh, yes," Anne said bitterly. "The car had to be fixed. Otherwise, why would that cop have asked me all those questions? I just figured it out."

Thunder broke over the house. Anne bounced to her feet and went to stand at the window.

"Oh, *I'd* have murdered somebody, if I'd known!" she said.

"Where were you?" I asked.

"That steak place next to Shakey's. Harry had his Bloomington meeting, and Ben came by that afternoon and said, why don't you meet me for dinner, nothing really special, Ellie's out of town—that's his girlfriend—and we'll both have company, at least."

"Ben?"

"My brother-in-law. You saw him at the funeral home."

"Oh, yes."

"So I drove up there. I was going to meet him at eight-thirty, but he was a little late, so I went into the bar for a drink. I'd just been served when he arrived. And then we sat over dinner and talked, about *nothing*...." She put her fists to her temples and shook her head. "Just *nothing*," she continued. "Until nearly midnight! And all the time, that monster was stalking my son not a hundred yards away! When I think of it...!" She turned to face us, fists still clenched, mouth tight.

"I'm sorry," I said. I tried to get up, but my legs weren't having any. Anne sat down again, across the table from me.

"Forgive me," she said. "It's been a bad year. My sister died last March, did I tell you?"

I nodded.

"I thought I had. She was seven years older than me and always... Oh, it was terrible." Tears spilled. She wiped them away with the back of her hand. "Poor Bob," she said, smiling at the boy. "It must be hard when the grownups go to pieces."

The kid smiled politely. He was already taller than me and pretty filled out; if he had much more growing to do, I'd be surprised.

"March is always the bleakest month anyway," Anne said. She looked at the kitchen clock, an antique wall clock on which the second hand jumped irregularly. "Goodness, almost eleven! I wish I had my car, J. J. I could run you back to your motel. Or, Bob?"

Bob shook his head. "I walked. I don't own a car, and since I got Dad's station wagon so muddy last week, I can't use any of his cars for the rest of the month."

"Oh?" I said.

"That's what we used to transport the saucer," he explained. "All that gear wouldn't fit in Dave's MG."

"Right," I said, astonished at myself for not having thought of that sooner.

I heard a sliding, bumping noise beyond the kitchen, and then a very quiet car engine. "Oh, good," Anne said. "Here's Harry, right on cue. Now he can take you both home, and you won't have to get wet."

A car door slammed in the garage, and a key fumbled into the kitchen-door lock. "Just a sec," Anne called. "The chain's on." She got up and went to the door. "Ben! Back so early?"

"Ellie wasn't feeling good," he said. "So I took her home. The heat, I think." He looked past Anne to the two of us at the table, pulling off his driving gloves finger by finger. "Oh, is it a party?"

Anne made perfunctory introductions. "I can take you all home now," she said.

"Don't bother with me," said Bob. "I don't mind a little rain. I can walk. But I'd better get going, or I'll be grounded."

"You're the UFO man," Ben said to me. "Mind staying a little longer? I'd like to talk to you."

Anne excused herself to let Bob out the front door. I heard them moving through the house, scraps of polite words, the door opening. Anne Streich's brother-in-law stared at me. "Look," he said. "I don't know what your game is, but believe me, you won't get any money out of this family. If I hear so much as a whisper that you might have tried, I go to the police. Is that clear?"

"The rain's letting up," Anne said, as she walked into the kitchen. Her brother-in-law looked up, startled into silence. Anne picked up the coffee pot and refilled my mug.

"I'll walk home," Ben said.

"Don't be silly—I can give you a ride," Anne assured him. "I'm taking J. J. back to his motel anyway."

"Motel! I thought you lived in town," he said.

"I had a fire," I explained. "And I can walk too, Anne. Excelsior Boulevard isn't the back of beyond."

"Sit still and drink your coffee," she replied. "Of course I'll give you a ride. Don't you be silly either. It's that one near the chicken place, isn't it?"

"I'm leaving." Ben started toward the back door. "And you," he said, pointing at me. "Remember what I just said." He snapped back the bolt and whipped through the door, giving it more of a slam than a door in a well-built house really needs.

Anne went to the door to turn the deadbolt. "Has he been threatening you?" she asked, sounding incredulous.

"Not really. He was just telling me not to bother to try to extort any money from you."

"Oh, how awful!" She laughed. "Poor Ben. He's just not used to having Paula's money, that's all. Makes him insecure."

I rearranged the Streich family in my head as I took another sip of coffee. "I never heard of money making people insecure," I said.

Anne gave me her sideways glance. "Of course it does," she said. "It's the richest men who have the strongest locks, isn't it?" She made money sound pretty undesirable.

I noted with mild interest that I was too tired to respond to the glance. "I'll have to go soon," I said.

"Finish your coffee. When Harry gets here, one of us will drive you." She pushed the little plate of cookies toward me. I shook my head, and she took one herself.

"You seem like the listening type," she said.

"Sometimes."

"Harry's not. He buries things. He doesn't want to talk about any of this—this business with David. Not that he's uncaring—I don't want you to think that. But he bottles things up, you know? Because he's afraid of his own feelings." She bit into the cookie. "And he does...odd things." That glance again. "Like sleeping in the guest room so it won't bother me when he can't sleep." She smiled, a tight smile. "Not that I can't hear him pacing anyway."

If it was a come-on, I wasn't about to do anything about it, so

[102]

I wrapped my hands around my mug and resigned myself to hearing some confidences. I wished she would turn on another light; the kitchen was lit, now, only by the light above the sink. The leaves of the herbs in the row of square clay pots looked transparent. Something about them made me feel transparent myself.

"Harry wouldn't even try to figure out who could have done this to David, if he had any idea about the car. I don't think he'd even listen long enough for me to tell him about it. But I want to know. Somebody who knew him? But who?"

"Who, indeed?" I murmured.

She finished the cookie. "Almost anybody," she mused. "After the spread that balloon stunt got in the newspapers, he had a reputation. The kids in school were still calling him Ufo last year! They never forget anything, kids. So somebody looking for help with a—a project like that might think of him."

And I was the one who had tracked the kid down, three years before. I looked up at her, but she was pushing back the cuticles on her left hand with her other thumbnail. I felt too guilty to say I was sorry.

"I wonder what kind of story he was told, to make it seem reasonable."

"We'll probably never know," I said.

"That's what scares me," Anne said in a faint voice. Now she did look at me, forehead creased. "Not ever knowing. Any of it."

"It's hard," I agreed. The coffee, good as it was, was beginning to upset my stomach, and my brain kept trying to shut off. I tried to think of something comforting to say, but my imagination had given up for the night. I wished Harry would come home.

"I shouldn't burden you with this," Anne said. "I'm sorry. But you see, Harry doesn't want anyone to know what Dave did that night, in case there were any damages, so I can't go to anyone else...." Her voice trailed off, and she put her hand to her forehead.

I was rescued by the shifting, sliding, bumping noise from the garage. *It must be the garage-door opener*, I thought. "There he is now," Anne said, and got up to let him in.

My coffee was long gone. Harry didn't look too pleased to see me, and after several minutes of strained conversation they agreed that since he was tired out from his meeting (what kind of meeting, every Friday night? I wondered), Anne would drive me back to the motel.

She gave the cream BMW a critical examination before she got in. "Ben borrowed it last night, too," she explained. "The slob brought it back all splashed up. I'm glad to see he's had it washed."

"Doesn't he have a car?"

"It's in for repairs. Has been all week. Thank God mine's never been out that long, except once when they had to get a part from Chicago. Just goes to show the Japanese haven't caught up with the Germans yet, no matter what the ads say."

"They make some decent cars," I said, impelled by a vague loyalty to Mack's Honda. I got into the BMW and let my head rest against the headrest. Much more comfortable than either the Honda or Mack's squad car, I reflected. An image of the dead girl rose up behind my closed eyelids, and I hastily opened them.

Anne drove as if the car were part of her lithe body, although how much of that was her own skill and how much the car's engineering, I couldn't tell. We hardly spoke as she turned toward Excelsior Boulevard, me because I was too tired to say anything, she perhaps sunk in her own painful thoughts. She let me out in the motel lot with a wan smile, turned the car in a tight U, and zipped away.

I had forgotten, I noticed with disgust, to pull the door of my room tight to the jamb. Serve me right if I lost everything, all hundred dollars' worth of it. I pushed the door open and fumbled to the right for the light switch.

No chance to find it. The back of my head exploded in pain. The floor rushed toward me, and everything went black.

# XII

BIRD. Singing bird.

Robin?

Very damp bed. And the bird somewhere very close. Robin. And another, farther away.

Wings beating above my head. A waterbird.

The smell was the smell of fields in spring, wet earth where worms are stirring.

The robin flew a little closer and sang some more, the irregular caroling unbearably cheerful. Under my eyelids, my eyes burned. And my head, my head had a pounding pain jumping through it.

That funny feeling in my stomach was a shiver. I felt pleased and proud that I had identified it, and its cause: my clothes were soaked through.

But where was I?

I distinctly remembered being driven back to my motel: the cream car turning in the bluish light of the parking lot, Anne Streich's little wave, like the queen of England's, as she nosed onto Excelsior Boulevard. I couldn't remember entering the room, or leaving it if I had entered. But wherever I was lying, it wasn't on the limp strings of the shag rug, and it wasn't on the purple plush bedspread.

Yet it was early morning, I knew without opening my eyes. When I did open them, my surmise was confirmed: the shadowless light of predawn illuminated the woodland I was lying in; in June in Minnesota, something before five in the morning.

The pale blotch I brought slowly into focus was my own left hand, a medium-sized hand with a few fine dark hairs on the backs of the fingers and the back of the hand itself, and my chunky white-gold wedding ring on the third finger. A loose fit, after all the jogging Karen had talked me into. Whoever had brought me here had not robbed me. The hand lay on a bed of brown, wet, half-decomposed leaves. That slimy thing I could feel under my first and second fingers was an old maple twig, a

[ 105 ]

rime of greenish white fungus growing on it. I thought about wiping my fingers on my pants, but it seemed like too much trouble to move. Instead, I closed my eyes.

There were other twigs scattered on the old leaves. I could feel them pressing into the right side of my chest, through my shirt. That whine was a mosquito. Probably already full of my blood. I wondered if I had lost blood to anything bigger than a mosquito but decided I was too comfortable as I was to investigate.

Perhaps a quarter mile away, a tiger roared.

*Sure,* I told myself. *A tiger, in Minnesota. Go back to sleep; you're already dreaming.*

*But there are tigers in Minnesota,* an insistent little voice told me. *Real tigers, roaming free, not so far from Minneapolis.*

*Hogwash,* I told the voice.

I reopened my eyes. *Just as an experiment,* I thought, *why don't you try moving that hand?* I thought about twitching my fingers. Somewhat to my surprise, the fingers twitched.

*Try sitting up,* I suggested.

*Not yet, not yet. Is this shock?* I wondered.

*If you are in shock, Joseph Jamison, and out in the middle of some woods, you had better do something about the situation. Like sitting up.*

That was more of a project than moving the hand, but I got myself erect and leaning against a chain-link fence that happened to be convenient to my back.

The pounding in my head got fiercer, and my forehead landed on my knees even though I tried to keep it up and look around me. I did get one of my hands onto the back of my head, to explore a throbbing spot. Very sore, the spot was.

Somebody must have hit me, I thought. I could almost remember it. Almost.

*Now, there's something odd,* I noticed. My wallet, with all its contents scattered about, including the business cards from CATCH, which lived in a little snapped pocket all their own. Slowly, I recognized that here was a problem I could do something about. I got my fingers working and gathered up my bits and pieces: driver's license, Visa card, cards from Dayton's and

Donaldson's department stores and the Amoco card I hadn't been able to find the other day and had accused Karen of losing, and the blue card from Montgomery Ward, hard to see against the still-dark leaves. I looked at them all and tried to think if anything was missing.

I discovered that I was sitting on my Blue Cross and AAA cards and added them to the ones already in my wallet. My sodden library card turned up stuck to the back of the Blue Cross card. I put the wallet into my left-hand back pants pocket, wet as it was, and felt extremely pleased with my performance.

The wet cards from CATCH were a dead loss. Biodegradable, so I left them on the ground.

The sun began to rise. A fresh breeze blew into my face as I leaned against the fence. Really, I thought, a very pleasant park or whatever. Various kinds of trees grew in this little woods, maple and oak and ash. I thought I saw some trillium blooming not too far away, although it was a little late in the season for that. I congratulated myself on remembering the season of the year. *Just a little while, now, while my head really gets working again*, I promised myself, *and I'll go for a little walk in this woods and look at the pretty flowers, and maybe figure out where I am.* People couldn't be too far away, I reasoned. Not with such a tall chain-link fence at my back.

The robin stopped singing. The tiger roared again, much closer.

*That's ridiculous, Joe. You're hearing things. Must be that blow on the head.* I turned the head in question and saw another chain-link fence, a few yards away and parallel to the one I was leaning on, and a dim recognition dawned.

I was twenty miles from the motel, in the Siberian-tiger enclosure at the Minnesota Zoo.

At the thought, my heart hammered without mercy at my head. I put my hands up and tried to hold my skull together.

I had been here once before, three years ago. Not *in* the enclosure, of course. On the path that goes past it, where the zoo visitors can stroll past and hope to catch a glimpse of the tigers. I tried to replay the memory: uphill on a broad, paved path. The tigers are on the right. You look down and see a stream.

Karen and I had been lucky: I had put the long lens on CATCH's Minolta and taken some semi-interesting pictures of a couple of tigers drinking and playing in the water. But the tigers don't sit around waiting for people to take their pictures. They roam around in their woods.

How many tigers?

I didn't have the faintest idea. Just tigers. There could be two. There could be twenty. No, probably not twenty. Certainly more than two. *Do tigers hunt in packs?* I wondered.

Not that it mattered. One, half-grown, would be more than a match for me, even at my best.

And I was definitely not at my best.

The sun had lifted into the branches of the trees to my left. Where was I in the enclosure? That was the important thing. If only I could think!

I tried to picture the lay of the land. There was a hill to the left of the stream in my picture, wasn't that right? And you walked on, and beyond the tigers was a place for water buffalo —no, musk oxen—and then the camels mixed in with the wild horses. O, for a wild horse to drag me from my fate!

*That feeling is panic, Joe. Stop it!* I had a momentary lucid image of one of the Bactrian camels, its supercilious lip and large, moist eyes.

Eyes. Linda had no eyes.

I shivered. Cold. *Joe, you could die sitting here, even without the tigers.*

You go around the curve. This part wasn't clear. The path curves to the right, and…moose, was it? And you keep on to the right, turn right at a T intersection, yes, that's it, there's a bunch of high, false rocks and a moat to keep the tigers in. I could get across that without any trouble, but I'd never get out on the other side, where I'd taken my pictures. That was a high fence, a steep climb. If I could just remember which direction the whole trail faced! Did you start out going north, south, east, west?

Wait. Northern Trek. The trail was called the Northern Trek. Unless Fate, in the form of zoo officials, was determined to be cruel, the trail must take a northward loop. I'd have to go east, then.

I took my left hand off skull-holding duty and looked at my watch. Five-fifteen. A faint crackling noise caught my attention: a tiger, going uphill to my right, away from me. At the sight, my bladder wanted to empty itself. *Don't pee now, Jamison. You'll have a tiger on your tail.*

Had the tiger gone over the crest of the hill, or had it only stopped? I peered and peered, but I couldn't be sure. And where were the others?

I began to appreciate the value of that burnished orange striped coat. Far from the gaudy hide it seemed, it was an almost perfect camouflage in this wooded tract. I thought wistfully of the orange handles of Karen's garden tools, so bright against our close-cropped lawn.

I stood up, slowly and carefully. The pain in my head increased as I stood, and settled back to a steady pulse as I leaned against the fence. The breeze was beautiful, soft, smelling of woodland. And, I realized, blowing in the one right direction for me, through the tigers' woodland, carrying my man scent to the musk oxen.

I would keep the fence at my back, I planned, encouraged. Work my way downhill, toward the brightening light. I wasn't sure what happened on the tigers' side of the fake rocks. Did the fence continue, or do tigers not climb? Was there a fence, hidden from the path, that kept the tigers out of the moat? I'd have to take my chances.

After several painful steps, I stopped. Should I climb the fence instead? I tilted my head back and looked at it; it seemed to continue infinitely toward the sky and the overhanging branches of the trees. Fifteen feet, at least. Topped with barbed wire. How high can a tiger jump? High enough to pull a clumsy man from a fence?

The pounding in my head increased, and my vision began to darken. I carefully returned my head to an upright position, and things cleared.

I put my left foot out to my left and shifted my weight onto it slowly. A twig snapped.

*How many tigers?*

Something was holding me back. My right hand, clawed into the fence. Sweating and shivering, I made it loosen. Had I been

[109]

put over that fence? I wondered. Not possible. I'd have broken half my bones when I fell.

When I thought about it, there was something wrong with my right leg. The pain in my head had distracted me from it before, but it wasn't holding me up the way it should.

A red-and-blue face. A man with a red-and-blue face put me here, I remembered. Something out of an old *National Geographic* came to mind, a brown, painted face with a bone through the nose and stiff, coarse fibers braided into the human hair. No. A ski mask. Pleased to have this bit of memory, I turned it over again and again.

Over the hill, the tiger, or another one, roared again. The robin was singing again too, a couple of trees farther away.

Wouldn't it be quiet with a tiger around?

*Stupid, tigers don't hunt robins.*

A kid had been mauled here at the zoo, I remembered. Not by a tiger, by one of the cats indoors, which had reached through the wire of its cage.... Well, but the cat had only been playing, and the kid had been inside the guardrail; it was his own damn fault.

You *are inside the guardrail, Joe.*

*Oh, yeah, I keep forgetting.*

Where was my adrenaline? I moved sideways along the fence, favoring my sore right leg. The mosquitoes had been at me in the night too. I soon had my forearms scratched pink.

*Stop it, Joe. Don't give the tigers any blood to smell.*

A wave of darkness. *I'm not going to make it,* I thought. *I'm going to fall down and get eaten by tigers and Karen will never understand why and the man in the red-and-blue ski mask will laugh. Big joke.*

Something burning in my throat. I remembered something burning in my throat. I almost coughed, remembering. The man in the ski mask holding something to my mouth. He must have given me something, I realized. Something to keep me knocked out until the tigers ate me. I felt a peculiar sort of gratitude toward the kind man in the ski mask who had been so thoughtful.

*Stop it, Joe.*

I looked back and saw my business cards scattered on the

[ 110 ]

ground. I had come almost fifteen feet. My heart took a joyous leap, and my left hand touched a rough surface.

The fence had run out. Well, but I could keep my back to the smooth side of the rock. And once around it, wasn't there a grassy slope and the moat and…and what? Sheer wall?

A steep bank. I was almost sure I remembered a steep bank. I remembered thinking, *How do they control the tigers in the winter, when the water freezes?*

My feet had got tangled in something. I looked down. Honeysuckle, in red bloom. Beautiful. Tears came to my eyes, that I should be granted this sight of honeysuckle. I looked back the way I had come and saw the tiger, or a tiger, walking among the trees maybe fifty yards away. Paying no attention to me. How dare he pay no attention? Doesn't he know there's a man on his turf?

I stopped the yell as it rose to my lips. More darkness, clearing slowly. *Keep going, Joe.* National Geographic *needs you. Or* Reader's Digest. *What a first-person story!* Karen would be so happy—she could write it for me and start her career. I thought of me sitting in the recliner in the family room, telling the story, and Karen doing the polishing and typing, and I congratulated myself on the brilliance of this idea, which had burst upon me as the theory of relativity must have burst upon Einstein. I had half the story outlined in my head before I came to what passed for my senses and looked down, to see that I was still standing in the sweet perfume of the honeysuckle. I moved on.

Later, I pressed my face into the damp, shaggy grass at the edge of the moat. There was no steep bank. Just the grassy descent to the orange water, and across the way, a few strokes away for a swimmer, a sheer wall.

The fake rock, though, was craggy. And I did have things tigers aren't blessed with: two hands with fingers, two feet with toes. I jammed my fingers into the highest crack I could reach and began to climb.

If I fell, I would smack my head again. Should I angle out across the wall, to fall into water?

*And drown, Joe?*

"Up" became a tropism, something I did, slowly, fearfully, but as automatically as a sunflower turns with the sun. And I, like that flower of Blake's my high-school English teacher was so fond of, was weary with time. Very weary. I almost wept at the poetry of the situation.

A tiger roared, very close.

I scrambled over the top, fell, rolled, clawed my way through a few young spruce trees and more honeysuckle, bumped my abused head into something very hard, and blacked out.

A zoo employee, readying the path for the day's visitors, found me draped over the guardrail.

This, I reconstruct. I remember the man's shocked face, the flush of anger as he realized that I had actually been inside the enclosure with the tigers.

"Those aren't house cats!" I remember him yelling. "They're wild animals! They're dangerous, even if you know what you're doing."

I remember somebody shaking me.

I remember being placed on some sort of small vehicle, something like a large golf cart, and taken to a room of some kind. Someone's office, I think.

I remember somebody holding a cup of tea to my mouth. Brown uniforms, a blanket draped over my shoulders and wrapped loosely around my body. I fingered the blanket, I remember, wondering if I had brought it with me from the motel. I couldn't quite see how I had done it.

Someone said something about arrest. I looked up. "The man with the red-and-blue face," I said, taking care to make the words very distinct.

"What man?" A brown face, close to mine.

"*National Geographic*," I explained, careful with the pronunciation. The face twitched in an angry frown and withdrew. "No," I said. "No."

"I think he needs a doctor," said a voice behind me.

Encourage that. "See my bump?" I let my head hang forward and tried to get my hand to the sore place on my skull, but something was holding my arm down. *They've tied me up*, I thought, panicking. *They think I'm a tiger; they're going to put me back in the cage.*

It was only the blanket, of course.

"Looks like he got hit on the head." The person behind me poked through my hair with what felt like a knife and was more likely a finger. "That's quite a bruise."

"Maybe when he went over the fence?"

"I don't think he did go over the fence," said the first person. "The barbed wire is all right, and he's not scratched up as far as I can see."

"Maybe he was dumped in," said the second. "Maybe we should get the police to look around."

I tried to nod at that, mumbled, "Yes, police."

"Oh, Christ," said the voice behind me. "That's all we need. Some nut running loose."

I thought they were talking about me.

Later still, I was riding again, in something bigger. Lying down, shivering. Somebody sitting beside me.

"Tell me how you got into the tiger enclosure," this person, male, dark blue, suggested.

"He had a blue nose."

"Mmmhmm. And a green chin?"

"No, red."

The person was quiet a few seconds. "A ski mask, maybe?"

I nodded, or tried to nod. My head hurt. "Can I have a couple of aspirin?"

"Not now."

"*Please!*" I tried to sit up. The person effortlessly pressed me back down.

"Just relax," he said. "We'll be at the hospital soon."

"What hospital?"

"Methodist, in St. Louis Park." He appeared to think this needed explanation. "You're going to have some special X rays on their machine there."

"My wife's there."

"Oh? She a nurse?"

"No." It was getting harder to talk again. I wanted just to go to sleep. "She had a baby."

"Okay. Just lie still. We'll be there soon."

[ 113 ]

"I found my Blue Cross card," I said proudly.

"Uh-huh. Lie down."

My eyes burned under the lids. A tiger was walking up a hill, roaring. It turned around and grinned at me through its ski mask. The tiger's aunt thought it was great to have *two* practical jokers in the family. She roared and roared. Mother was angry. A man with a bone in his nose climbed onto the back of the tiger. Man from Niger. Inside the tiger. Smiling tiger.

"I'm not from Niger," I said plaintively.

"Soon, soon," soothed the man. "Real soon. Feel that little sway, there? We just got onto the crosstown. We'll be there in just a few minutes."

I sneezed. My head exploded.

A tiger with a napkin around its neck advised me to eat my breakfast, hungry or not.

"Just a cookie, thanks," I said.

"What are they looking for back there?" The man's voice was raised for someone else. I couldn't hear the reply. "Tell them to look for a red-and-blue ski mask. Last night was too damn hot to wear one for long. Maybe he took it off and dropped it, if we're lucky."

"I'm a lucky man," I said.

"That's the first thing you've said all morning that completely made sense."

I opened my eyes and looked at the person in blue beside me. "We're here," he said, standing up.

"Hi, Mack," I said, filled with recognition. "How's tricks?"

The guy grinned down at me. "Just fine. Only my name's not Mack."

Aboard the flying saucer, a humanoid in a white coat smiled at me. She had a long, thin face and a long, thin nose, a deep tan, and small, dark eyes. "Hold very still," she said. "If you move, you'll spoil the picture."

Strange, padded objects moved into view. The humanoid adjusted them carefully to my head, pressed against my cheekbones. "These will help you hold still," s⟩ ⟩ said. "Just breathe quietly and evenly and don't move your h ⟩ ⟩." She smiled again. When she smiled, she looked almost ⟩⟩⟩⟩⟩ ⟩kay?"

[ 114 ]

I think I said, "Okay."

A Venusian, maybe. Or some sort of being from Titan, that moon of Saturn's that has an atmosphere. A robot, it would have to be, of course, because how could the creatures themselves breathe our air? But an extraordinarily realistic robot. "Extraordinary," I said.

"Shh. Hold still."

The robot went away. Rolling just my eyes, I caught a glimpse of a squarish, softly lit room, with what appeared to be viewports off to one side, through which I could see a whitish figure moving. Perhaps one of the aliens?

My belly lurched as the slab I was lying on began to move, projecting my head into a ring-like device I thought I recognized from descriptions given by other abductees. The slab, made of some marvelously comfortable but firm alien material, stopped. *Whirr-clunk!* the machine said. *Whirr-clunk, whirr-clunk, whirr-clunk!* Though I tried my hardest to keep track, I lost count of the number of times the ring made its noise. Many. Fifty or sixty.

Some investigator you are, Jamison, I could almost hear Prunella Watson saying over the phone from headquarters. If the aliens let me return to my earthly life.

The slab moved a fraction of an inch. Half a centimeter, I would try to remember to tell CATCH, which is on the metric system. The ring spoke again. And again, when it fell silent, the slab moved. I fought my heavy eyelids. In vain.

I woke as the slab returned to its original position. I sneezed, and froze in fear. "That's okay," the smiling humanoid assured me. "We were all done with that part. Want to blow your nose?"

"No," I said, touched by the alien's concern. My voice seemed very weak. Perhaps some of the paralysis reported by some other abductees.

"Sure? Okay. Now, we're going to do this once more, only this time we're going to inject something into your arm that won't let the X ray through, understand?"

"Are the proteins compatible?" I asked. "We may be different, here on earth."

She hesitated, looked at me carefully. "That's okay," she said. "It won't hurt you." I felt a prick in my left arm. "Just hold still now. This might feel cold."

It did. She went away. The slab moved.
The ring spoke.

"Feeling better?"

I know this man: my own doctor. "Not too bad." I put my hand to my forehead. "I've got one hell of a headache."

He looked at the papers in his hand. "I can't say I'm surprised. It should wear off pretty soon, though. Where did you get that bump on your head?"

"I'm not sure, but I think somebody hit me when I walked into my motel room last night."

His eyebrows shot up. "How come you were in a motel room?"

"Somebody set fire to my house."

The eyebrows went up again, higher this time. "You do have troubles. Fortunately, no brain damage, though. The CAT scan was normal."

"CAT scan?"

"That special X ray," he explained. "Don't you remember it? The technician's note says you were alert and cooperative."

"Oh." *Humanoid, Jamison? Robot?* Plain human being, that girl was. Talk about far gone! But at least I would have no deficiencies as an investigator to confess to Prue Watson.

"I think you're a little disoriented from a combination of fatigue, exposure, and the blow to the head," the doctor said. "Rest should be a good cure. I'm keeping you here for a while, though, to see how things go." He looked as if he had wanted to ask another question and had thought better of it. "Karen and Joey are fine, you'll be glad to know. Karen can come down and see you later on."

"What time is it?"

He glanced at his watch. "A little after two."

I looked up at the ceiling, where there were tracks for curtains to be pulled around the bed. One curtain had been pulled part way. "I must have slept some," I said.

"Good for you. The more, the better." He looked back at the chart, flipped a page. "Oh, and you've got a bad bruise on your

[ 116 ]

right leg. It's been X-rayed, and there's no fracture, so it looks like you lucked out on that, too."

"Good," I said, since it seemed to be expected of me.

"Favor it, if you can," said the doctor. Giving me a friendly squeeze on the bad right leg, he left the room.

# XIII

WHEN I woke again, I had a visitor: Chelon.

The sergeant sat with his feet planted firmly on the floor in front of him and his hands clasped between his knees, his usual slow-blinking gaze studying my face. Probably what had wakened me, I thought.

"Are you coherent?" he asked.

What a question! "I think so."

"Care to tell me what you were doing out there with the tigers?"

"Trying to get away without attracting any attention."

"Don't get smart with me, Jamison." Blink. "Somebody's trying to kill you, and I don't like the way they go about it." Blink. "Too cute."

"I'm getting used to it," I said.

Blink. "So I hear. Want to tell me about the others?"

I told him about the accident I'd had in the parking lot at work and finding that the brake line of my car had been nicked. He blinked. I told him about the tan Rabbit that had kept me hopping over most of the Linden Hills neighborhood.

"Tan Rabbit," he said, his mouth puckering into a tight line. "You got any idea how many Rabbits are registered in the Twin Cities? And not one of them to anybody connected with this case. I've checked out every last person at that funeral, everybody who signed the book at the funeral home, all Amant's known associates in this area, and let me tell you, that man got around—" He broke off, shaking his head, then stared at me. "It did have Minnesota plates, didn't it?"

I thought about that, closed my eyes to try to see the car as it followed me down Xerxes to the Thumb, in the lot as I came out. "I think so," I told Chelon. "At least, they were the right color; I'm sure about that."

"You didn't get the number."

"No."

Chelon sighed. "Well, the color's something. So this guy has tried to get you three times."

"Four."

Blink. "Four? How do you figure that?"

"The fire in my house. Set right outside my bedroom window, with the fan pulling air into the room."

This time he didn't blink. "I never heard about that."

"Mack didn't tell you?"

"Not yet." I got the impression that Mack would be telling him, in detail, very soon, whether he wanted to or not. "You try."

So I told him about the call from Linda—

"Eileen," Chelon corrected.

—and getting home from the hospital to find my house burned. "I thought all this had been checked out. Mack said I was covered for the whole evening."

"Yeah, but that wasn't about any fire."

Oh. Because the girl had got herself killed. "That was just because she turned up dead," I said.

"After she called you."

"I certainly hope so."

Blink. "You're getting to be a regular Typhoid Mary," he commented. "Got any ideas why anybody should want to get rid of you?"

"Never happened before I found that body Saturday," I said. "So I guess that's where it started, though I'm damned if I can see why."

"What happened before the brake line? You were in Chicago the two days before; then you came back and went straight to that kid's funeral. Anything else?"

"Uhhh...no. I don't think so.... Wait. Somebody did call me at work. Or I returned his call."

"Who was that?"

"That guy from Purchasing..." My head wasn't perfect yet. I couldn't remember the name.

"Hudson?"

"Yeah, him. Wanted to know why I had sicked the cops on him. And he kind of pumped me about Amant, like there was something he wanted to know and thought I would come through with." I hesitated, then decided not to tell him what Pedersen had learned. I was pretty sure Pedersen wouldn't want his talents advertised, and I was damn sure I wasn't going to claim them for myself.

"Anything else?"

"I just remembered. Somebody called me and asked if I owned a blue Fairmont. Then he hung up."

"Could it have been Hudson?"

I tried to recapture the sound of the voices. "Maybe. Whoever it was, was trying to disguise his voice, I thought. Or else somebody had him by his private parts."

"You." Chelon had produced a notebook, seemingly out of thin air, and was scribbling in it. I didn't know whether to laugh. "And the Rabbit?" he asked. "When was that?"

"That same day. I took a cab home after work, after the accident. It was late, so I rode my bike over to the convenience store on 43rd to pick up something fast for supper. I noticed the Rabbit behind me then, but it wasn't until I came out of the store that he really started chasing me."

"He?"

I shrugged. "It could have been a woman, I guess."

"You didn't report it? To the Minneapolis police?"

"What could I report?" I remembered Mack asking the same question. "I hadn't seen the driver or the license plate—I was keeping track of him in the little rearview mirror I've got on my handlebar. It's not big enough to show a whole car, not that close."

"If it had to be an animal, it could have been a Jaguar, at least," Chelon said, still writing. "Those Rabbits. I think they breed them." Now I knew I should laugh, but I didn't have it in me. "Could he have been watching your accident, maybe? So he knew it didn't work?"

"I guess so."

"Unless you've got two people after you." Chelon nodded slowly, blinking once. "I like that. I like that. It makes things a lot simpler. Now, what about that fire?"

"The fire," I repeated. My head was pounding again. "I told you about Linda—Eileen calling. Mack seemed to think she called to set me up to get killed in the fire. Now that, I can't figure."

Chelon shook his head. "What do you think about it? Did she set you up?"

"It looks that way, if you just look at the call," I admitted. "But I can't make it fit with the other things she did. Like giving me the envelope, asking me to go to the police with it."

A nurse popped her head into the room, looked severely at Chelon, who stared her down, and withdrew. I wondered what had happened to the roommate I had been fuzzily aware of earlier that day: the other bed was flat and smooth.

"Go on," Chelon prompted. "What did she say?"

"She said she wanted to tell me something else, or something like that. She wanted to see me. Come over, that was it. Mack was taking me back to you with the envelope, so I told her I was going back out and wouldn't be home until eleven."

"*Back* out?"

"She'd been trying to get me for a while." I closed my eyes and wondered if Chelon would let me sleep some more soon.

"Did she come over at eleven?"

"No. I mean, I have no idea. She could have. That was the night Karen went into labor, remember? And I never did get home." Only two nights ago? It had to be longer, didn't it? But try as I might, I couldn't come up with any more days to put in between.

"Any word from Hudson all that time?"

"No. But I don't see why he should call again. He already knew I didn't know anything."

"Or weren't saying."

What was it Hudson had said? *I can see you aren't talking,* something like that. Or was I remembering that only because Chelon had suggested it?

"Something wrong?" Chelon asked.

"That girl bothers me," I said truthfully. "Why would she give me that envelope and then start a fire? Only it was a man that started the fire, now that I think of it. My neighbor saw him running away."

"Maybe she wanted to get rid of you, and the envelope along with you."

I stared at Chelon while I considered that. "Amant's girl?" I asked.

"That's right, I keep forgetting." Blink. "What would you say if

[ 121 ]

I told you our friend Eileen had nothing to do with Amant?"

I remembered the slender hands on the cigarettes never smoked, the sandwich never eaten, with the strap marks of the purse pressed into the fingers. "That wasn't her story," I said.

"He didn't have anything about her on him. Not a note, not a picture, not a phone number."

"He could have carried her phone number in his head," I pointed out. "That's what I'd do, if I wanted to keep an affair a secret. And he did. He gave his girl some line about an invalid wife."

"Amant wasn't even married."

"So he had some other reason."

"He did have a girlfriend, though." Chelon watched my face without blinking. "Had a picture of her on the dresser in the motel. Some dishwater blonde, older than this chick by a good twenty years."

"So he had two," I said. People don't turn pale on demand, swallow before every sentence without reason. "Wouldn't be the first guy on earth."

"And a lot of hot notes. Signed L."

"L for Linda."

"Name was Eileen, remember?"

"So maybe she liked Linda better and used that. She wouldn't be the first woman who hated the name she was given. My sister-in-law's name is Deborah, and everybody calls her Ginger. She's even got it on her charge accounts."

Chelon grinned. An unpleasant sight. "You just don't want to admit that kid had you fooled, that's your trouble, Jamison. Well, my time's up," he added, nodding at the nurse, who had reappeared and stood in the doorway with her hands on her hips. "I'll be in touch."

He got up, shook down his pants legs—even the hospital's air conditioning hadn't completely cowed the stickiness of the day —and moved to the door, where he looked back.

"Oh, by the way. This Eileen?"

"Linda," I said.

"Have it your way." Chelon blinked, slowly. "She was an actress. Supposed to be a damn good one. If it makes you feel any better, she was twenty-seven." He stepped through the door, chuckling, and was instantly out of sight. The nurse smiled at me and followed.

Had I known him personally? Linda had wanted to know. In other words, am I making a damn fool of myself? I sighed and wondered when Karen would put in an appearance. I needed to talk to somebody who said what they meant.

She arrived soon, but not soon enough, looking fresh and cheerful with her hair pulled back with a ribbon. The flowered housecoat was belted around a waist that was definitely a waist, even if it wasn't any twenty-two inches.

"Hi," I said, shinnying up in the bed on my elbows. We spent a minute or two in glad reunion, and then it occurred to me that the last time I had seen the housecoat, it had been hanging on the back of the bathroom door.

"Where did you get that?" I asked, pulling at the flowered belt.

Karen rescued her modesty with a slap. "This?" She looked puzzled. "I've had it almost three years, Joe. Don't tell me this is the first time you've noticed it!"

"Oh, come on," I protested. "I'm not that bad! I mean, how did it get to the hospital?"

"I gave Joy Forrester my key, and she got my stuff for me. Everything else was packed."

Chastened, because I'd never thought to ask her if she needed anything from home, I asked, "She didn't happen to notice anybody hanging around, did she?"

Karen laughed. "She didn't say so, and I didn't ask. I had other things to think about."

"I guess so," I said, smiling at her.

"I wanted to bring Joey down with me, but they wouldn't let me," she said, smiling back.

"I'll come up, as soon as I'm up to it, if that's okay. You look tired."

"You should see yourself." She took my hand and patted it. "I've got some good news, though. Mrs. Eskew called this morning. She invited us to use her spare bedroom until the house is fixed, and I took her up on it."

[ 123 ]

"That's a help." I shinnyed back up in the bed some more. "I've been wondering what we'd do about finding us a place, with me in here."

"How long will you be here, did the doctor say?"

"Long enough to rest."

"I'll let you do it, then." She'd been sitting on the edge of the bed. She got up and went to the door, smiling at me over her shoulder.

Joey. I'd seen my son exactly twice: he didn't seem quite real, even though Karen's belly was a third the size it had been on Thursday. I clamped my jaw on a wave of rage. Somehow, I promised myself, I was going to get that jerk. Not because he'd murdered Victor Amant. Not because he'd murdered Linda–Eileen. Not even because he'd murdered Dave Streich, a kid I'd known and liked. Because I resented having my own life interfered with every time I turned around.

Not too noble, maybe, but that's how I felt.

I had one other visitor on Saturday: Mack, who took my motel key and got me some clean clothes. Well, cleaner than the filthy stuff I'd worn Friday, anyway. The next day, Sunday, the whole Jamison family was cleared for release. I got dressed in the semiclean clothes and went downstairs to attend to the bookkeeping, then took the elevator up again to pick up Karen and Joey. I'd already called Mrs. Eskew, to let her know we'd be coming, and thanked her profusely. It'd be great to be right next door, where I could keep an eye on my own house.

I stepped off the elevator almost into the arms of the irascible doctor I'd crossed with a week before.

"I know you," he said. "Didn't I tell you not to bother the patients here? And you're too late, anyway. Anyone who was here a week ago is gone by now, so you can turn yourself right around and get back on that elevator before I call security."

"I'm here to pick up my wife and son," I said, and pushed past him.

"Don't you start asking questions, Jamison," he said to my back, somehow making his voice carry without raising it. "I'm checking, you understand? Harass these women, and you'll hear about it. Legally."

I turned and gave him the finger, but the elevator had already swallowed him up.

Mrs. Eskew came fluttering down her front walk as the cab pulled up in front of her house, twittering excitedly. A good neighbor is a prize beyond compare: I hadn't anticipated how gratifying it would be to have someone welcome us and exclaim over the baby.

And exclaim she did. "Oh, so small!" she chirped. "You forget how small they are when they're new. But such a *darling!* I believe he has your forehead, J. J."

I ran a hand over my receding hairline and tried to look proud. "May I carry him?" Mrs. Eskew took the baby from Karen without waiting for an answer and tucked him into an expertly crooked elbow. "So light! How much does he weigh?"

"Six and a half pounds," Karen said. "He's lost a little."

"Don't let it worry you," Mrs. Eskew said, bouncing up her front steps. "They all do."

Inside, it became apparent that Mrs. Eskew had been preparing for us ever since Karen had talked to her: a clean sheet had been tucked over the red plush of her couch ("Babies do spit up," she said over her shoulder, where a diaper had miraculously appeared under Joey's small forehead); the dining-room table was set for a meal; the refrigerator proved crammed with goodies; and a mobile hung over the kitchen table ("I thought you might want to change him there")!

"Sit, sit, sit," the old lady twittered. We sat.

All in all, a calm and cheering interlude in the jungle hunt my life had lately become. It couldn't last.

I could have made it last a little longer, if I'd known. But no, I had to go tromping over to check my house, not half an hour after we'd been fed and coffeed by Mrs. Eskew.

The place had been ransacked.

"Kids," said the burly cop who came to look at the mess. "Some neighbor kid, for sure."

[125]

"How can you tell?"

"Look at what they boosted." He pointed to the empty spaces. "Portable color TV, that's a favorite. Amplifier, rock records, beer." He bent over and picked Leontyne Price up off the floor and put the record box on the coffee table. "See? That's no way to treat a lady."

I didn't tell him a cop had dropped her there; I just answered a few questions and fled, to try to recapture the spoiled peace next door.

Kids. Damn them! Well, at least they'd left me *Tosca*.

# XIV

"JAMISON, I've got a proposition for you."

I made a noncommittal noise into the telephone. Pedersen rocked back in his chair and looked on with interest. He'd taken the call, so he knew I was talking to Chelon.

"This guy of ours that has such an interest in you."

"I wish he were the only one!" That was for Pedersen. "Go on."

"What do you mean, the only one?"

Pedersen tented his fingers and smiled, a little semicircular smirk. I turned my back on him. "Oh, some kids ripped a piece of plywood off my house and stole my TV and my amplifier and a bunch of records and five cans of Old Milwaukee 3.2 beer."

"You sure it was kids?"

"That's what the cops said."

Chelon didn't say anything for a minute or two. "Yeah, it sounds like kids," he said cautiously. "You sure nothing else was missing?"

Pedersen made a clucking noise.

"Nothing I could see." I sneaked a sideways glance at Pedersen. He still had his head cocked to one side. Sometimes I think the guy can hear the other end of the conversation *through* my head. "I guess we just didn't have anything else worth stealing."

"What makes you say that?" Chelon asked.

"Because they went through the place and didn't take anything else. Not even my fancy calculator."

"The place had been searched, you're saying?"

"Unh-huh."

Pedersen folded his arms and gave me a look of mock severity. He hadn't heard this part of the story yet—or of the episode at the zoo, either, for that matter. I was keeping quiet about it, the zoo was keeping quieter than a mute swan, the cops weren't saying a word, and all of us were perfectly happy being clams.

Chelon had been silent a moment. "That doesn't sound like kids," he said. I could imagine him blinking. "But it gives me hope. Yes. It gives me hope."

"Why is that?"

"I started to put a proposition to you," he said. "Now I think it has a better chance of working. I want you to put an ad in the *Star*. Better have it in the *Tribune*, too. Offering to trade that envelope for cash, to be negotiated."

"You're the one with the envelope," I objected.

"I don't think our guy knows that, though. Or he wouldn't have bothered to go through your house."

"You think it was him? You don't think it was kids?"

Pedersen nodded, the semicircular smirk in place.

"No, I don't," said Chelon. "I think whoever did that was trying to make it look like kids. But what kid is going to bother carrying away five cans of 3.2 beer? They can hang around outside some supermarket and get some yoyo to buy some for them. Now, if it was bourbon..."

"I didn't have any."

"Too bad. I bet you could have used it. Well, listen..."

I listened, and Pedersen almost crawled into my lap and listened. I had some protests, but Pedersen egged me on, and finally I agreed to the arrangements Chelon wanted. I hung up, and Pedersen scooted his chair back to his desk, eyes shining.

"What do you think of that?" I asked.

"It sounds workable," he said. "Now, if I knew where to get at the police records..."

"I think they keep them on paper," I said.

He pulled the corners of his mouth down briefly. "I might have known. Medieval types. Like that calculator your discriminating thief did not take. No point in it, then."

The calculator was only three years old, but that's medieval, in computer terms, so I let it slide. I looked up the number for the *Star* and *Tribune* want ads, got myself an outside line, and dialed.

The ad, as dictated to me by Chelon, was to read as follows:

ENVELOPE—marked EVIDENCE. Yours?
Will sell. Call for terms. Joseph Jamison.

I dictated it just that way myself, to the girl who was careful to take all the information necessary for billing me, and had her read it back.

"No telephone number?" Pedersen asked.

"It's in the book."

"This is what you call 'smoking him out,' is it not?"

"Yeah," I said. "If I can get enough smoke out of a few scraps of paper."

"Soak them in lard," suggested Pedersen, the font of all knowledge.

I tossed him for coffee and lost. If it hadn't been my own quarter, I'd have suspected him of fixing it somehow. Maybe I did anyway. Other people do their tossing in public, in front of the machine.

I took off a little early to pick up my car, which was finally ready. And then I went home—or next door to home—to explain Chelon's scheme to Karen. I wasn't looking forward to that part.

I parked in my own garage and cut across the yard to Mrs. Eskew's. The carpenters had already started on the house. The naked skeleton of the new wall and roof were covered with cloudy plastic. I peered through it to be sure they had blocked the bedroom door as I'd asked, pulled up the edge of the plastic to see that they had replaced the charred rim joist as agreed, and went over to Mrs. Eskew's to face the music.

Karen reacted much as you might think. She started shaking her head before I was halfway through describing Chelon's plan, and she didn't stop.

"I don't like it," she said, a trifle redundantly. "You'd be a decoy. What if you got shot? He's shot two people already."

"Chelon thinks he threw the gun away."

"What makes him think that? He kept it the first time, didn't he?"

"Chelon thinks he thought he was done—because he thought we were in the house, and we'd be killed and the house and the envelope would be gone."

Karen shuddered and looked toward the bassinet, where Joey was sleeping in lacy splendor provided out of Mrs. Eskew's attic, a repository that resembles the Smithsonian Institute. "That's what I mean. The man's crazy."

"Chelon says that's why he threw me in the tiger enclosure—because he didn't have the gun any more, and he doesn't want to kill with his own hands."

Karen shook her head, a quick tremor as if she'd had a bad chill. "I think it was revenge. I think he thought you'd wake up in there and be hunted down. If he'd just wanted you dead, there are plenty of lakes he could dump you in."

"You're both wrong," Mrs. Eskew said, putting an enormous dish of ham salad on the table. "He's putting it up to fate, don't you see? To decide whether you'll be killed or just scared off."

"Let's not worry about the man's reasons now," I said. "And Chelon says he'll provide a bulletproof vest."

"The other two got shot in the head."

There wasn't much I could say to that. "I can't back down now," I said.

"Sure you can."

"Karen, I've got a score to even too."

She raised her hands a couple of inches and let them drop into her lap. *Go ahead*, the gesture said, *but don't say I didn't warn you.*

The ad wouldn't appear until morning, when the *Star* hits the streets at nine-thirty or so, so that night I spent with Karen and Joey. They each said about the same number of words to me.

I'd given Chelon a bit of an argument about going back to the motel, but he pointed out that the telephone company was still forwarding my calls, and if the killer had tried my phone before, it would look less suspicious if the same arrangement turned up. He had some equipment from the telephone company that would let him listen in on my calls, some kind of gadget that traced whatever incoming calls there might be, a recorder, and an answering machine into which I dictated a message that I would be back at six-thirty that evening. We got all that set up before I went to work the next morning. The telephone-company technician wished us luck, and I drove to the plant feeling very thoughtful, though not much was going through my head.

[130]

Pedersen salivated over me all day and even bought me a cup of coffee without tossing for it. I found the air conditioning rather cool, for a change. At least, I shivered every so often.

I filled my gut with a submarine sandwich from a takeout place, wished I hadn't, and reported to my motel room right on schedule. Chelon arrived ten minutes late, which did nothing to increase my sense of security.

He hadn't been there thirty seconds before the telephone rang. I looked at him.

"So answer it," he said, sounding exasperated.

"Hello?" I said.

"Is this the gentleman with the envelope for sale?"

I sat down on the purple bedspread, heart pounding. My mouth was suddenly dry. I worked up a little spit and said, "Yes, it is."

"Well," said this turkey, "I'm a writer, and I'm interested in odd personals ads. Would you mind explaining to me what your ad is all about?"

I looked at Chelon. He nodded. "Yes," I said. "I would." I hung up.

"You get a few," Chelon said. I wondered how often he did this kind of thing.

Chelon laid out a solitaire game that involved two decks of cards and a lot of twisting the columns around to fit on the narrow shelf the motel provided for writing. I went to the bathroom.

I came out. The phone rang. I answered it without prompting this time.

"What do you want for the envelope?" the velvet voice inquired.

"What's it worth to you?"

Chelon started wigwagging. I'd left out part of my spiel. But my caller saved me. "What's in it?" he asked.

"You tell me."

"I don't have the faintest idea." The velvet voice was starting to sound familiar. "I'm guessing it has something to do with the Amant murder, because you're the guy who found the body."

[131]

I thought I recognized the voice now. "Oh," I said. Chelon rolled his eyes toward heaven. He must have guessed what was coming.

"Mr. Jamison, this is Justin Hugbetter of Channel 7 News, as you've probably guessed." He had precisely the same tone of voice as the guy who makes cash calls for a local radio station. "I'm prepared to pay you two hundred dollars for that envelope."

"Wonderful," I said. "I'll record your bid and let you know when the auction's over."

"Three hundred. I'll give you two just for a description of the contents."

"Forget it."

"Mr. Jamison—"

I hung up.

"Christ," Chelon said. "Couldn't you have picked a classier place to stay? I could use some room service."

The phone rang.

"Jamison? Hugbetter. Five hundred, and that's my limit."

Chelon took the phone. "Hugbetter?" he growled. "That envelope is for sale only to the person who knows what's in it." I could hear Hugbetter chortle as he hung up.

"You should have asked him to bring you whatever it is you want," I said, stretching out on the bed.

"We should have brought a coffeepot," Chelon said. "I need a transfusion." I imagined him flipping for coffee with Pedersen and smiled. He sat down in the one chair the motel provided and flipped on the TV. "Who would have thought those guys read the personals?"

"My wife never misses them," I said.

Chelon found a rerun of *Starsky and Hutch* and settled down to make snide comments about it. I got out some of the work I had brought "home" and spread it out on the bed. I figured the company had had about six hours' good work from me in the past week, and though I have an understanding supervisor, there are limits.

Starsky and/or Hutch, in a miracle of fast driving, had just chased a felon out of the side of a parking ramp at about the fifth level, when the phone rang again. Chelon jerked and turned the sound down.

"Joe? Anything yet?"

"Not yet, honey."

Chelon slumped.

"I'll get off the phone then," Karen said. "I love you." Her voice trembled.

"I love you, too. Everything's going to be okay, don't worry."

Chelon turned the sound back up as I hung up. "Couldn't she call during an ad?" he complained.

"I'll suggest it next time."

By nine-thirty I had finished the work I had brought along and Chelon had switched to a baseball game. We watched bleakly as the Twins blew a three-run lead.

"Sometimes I think I bring them bad luck, just by watching," Chelon remarked. "Every time I see them, they're losing."

"That's not you," I said.

They lost, eleven to six. The news was over and I was half-asleep, when the phone rang again. I jumped.

"Answer it," Chelon ordered, his face taut.

"Jamison," I said.

"You have the envelope." High, squeaky voice. I wondered if the guy had seen the same spy movie I had, in Hopkins. Not the same showing I'd seen, of course. He had been busy elsewhere. I nodded at Chelon. It was the same voice that had asked if I owned a blue Ford Fairmont.

"What envelope is that?" I asked.

"The one you advertised." The guy's voice broke.

"I do have an envelope," I said. "Are you sure it's the one you want?"

"I think so."

"Tell me what's in it."

Chelon had made fists on his knees and was staring at me. "Some pictures," the voice said. "And…and a bag. A copy made out of a book."

Good enough. "I think we're talking about the same one."

"What do you want for it?"

[ 133 ]

"What's it worth to you?" I felt a bit of *déjà vu* at the words and wondered crazily if it could be Hugbetter calling back with a good guess.

"One thousand dollars," the voice said, sounding final.

Chelon pointed up. "Fifteen hundred," I said.

"You do know what it means then," the voice said. Chelon shook his head frantically.

"I don't have the slightest idea," I said. "But I know you want it badly."

Chelon smiled at me. Good boy.

"You're a bastard, Jamison," the caller said.

"Fifteen hundred." James Bond has nothing on me.

A deep sigh. "All right. Where?"

"The parking lot at Knollwood Plaza," I said. This was Chelon's spot: late at night, it would be nearly empty, and wide open so the guy couldn't duck away. Yet it gave him a place to station his men, in the building and in a few parked cars and vans.

"No good." The voice was showing signs of strain. I looked at Chelon's tape recorder and wondered whether it had been activated. I couldn't tell.

"It's going to be where *I* want it," the caller said. "You got your price."

Chelon nodded: *Don't lose him,* he mouthed.

"Let's hear it," I said.

"You know where Methodist Hospital is?"

Did I know where Methodist Hospital was! I almost hung up. "Yes," I said. It didn't come out as sarcastic-sounding as I'd intended.

"Go past it, headed west. First light is Louisiana. Just past that, close, is a right turn, Meadowbrook Boulevard. Park your car headed north on Meadowbrook, and come back out to the bus stop on Excelsior. We'll make the trade there. I don't get out of my car."

Chelon shook his head, pantomimed a door opening. "Why not meet in the middle of the street? Halfway?" I asked.

"No."

Chelon started dealing imaginary cards and pointed at me. You're the dealer, he meant, I guessed.

"Halfway, or forget it," I said, slapping my ace on the table. "I'll turn the envelope over to the police."

"Oh, all right," the voice said. "It doesn't make that much difference. Be there in half an hour."

Chelon shook his head: he needed time.

"I can't get it tonight," I said, glad we'd prearranged this part. "It'll have to be tomorrow."

"Tomorrow night, then. Around eleven."

Chelon nodded. "Okay," I said. "What kind of car do you have?" Chelon's camouflage question.

The bastard chuckled. "I think you know." He hung up.

Chelon flexed his fingers out of their fists, stood up, and scratched his ribs. "One for him, one for me," he said.

"How's that?"

"He chose that place because it's *right* on the city line. But that's a warren of apartment buildings. I could hide an army in there." He yawned. "Thank God that's over. Now I can go home."

I had a different thought. "Imagine being able to put your hands on that much money with no advance notice," I marveled.

Chelon half grinned. "You don't think he intends to bring any money with him, do you?" he asked. "Put that chair under the doorknob when I'm gone, will you?"

He left.

Ten minutes and a quick call to Karen later, I was asleep.

# XV

THE next afternoon, I kept an eye out for the tan Rabbit as I drove to the motel from work. I saw a couple, but they didn't seem to have any particular interest in me. Neither did anyone else, which was worrying. Chelon had told me I would have an escort. I complained about it when I called in.

"You eat yet?" was his response.

"No."

"Get something, quick, and then stay put in that room until it's time to go."

I drove down Excelsior to the Miracle Mile shopping center and picked up a takeout at the Chinese restaurant there, stopped in B. Dalton and bought a couple of magazines, and went back to the motel room. As arranged, I called in.

"Just a sec," Chelon said. Like most such seconds, his stretched out for several minutes. "Nobody visited while you were gone," he reported.

"Did you get that call traced?" I asked.

"Pay phone. In Southdale. Might as well have called from the North Pole. I'll see you later, okay?"

"Okay."

Nice to know somebody was keeping an eye on me, anyway. I polished off some acceptable moo goo gai pan, put away an egg roll that had turned a little chewy as it cooled, and cracked a fortune cookie that assured me "success with undertakers." I wasn't quite sure how to interpret that. Chalk it up to Oriental English, I decided, and take it as a good omen.

I called Karen. "So far, so good, honey."

"Oh, Joe, I wish you weren't doing this," she said. "I'm so *scared!* And Mrs. Eskew says the tension isn't good for my milk."

"Have a beer," I said. "I'll call you the minute it's over."

"Joe—"

"It's got to be done," I said, giving her the pep talk Pedersen had given me. "We can't just let the guy go around murdering people."

She didn't say anything. I could hear my new son fussing in the background. "Go take care of Joey," I said. "I'll be there by midnight, so don't fret. How are the carpenters doing?"

"They finished the roof today. The shingles don't really quite match, but I guess they'll do. And it has windows, now. And they put that black paper over the... What do you call it? Sheathing?"

"Sheathing."

"Anyway, outside will be done tomorrow, if the weather holds. He said another week."

"We could move back in and sleep on the hide-a-bed until they're done," I said. "Now, go take care of Joey."

"Okay. I love you."

"I love you too." I hung up and almost said the hell with the whole thing. Why should I, ordinary citizen and computer engineer, be cavorting around in a bullet-proof vest in the middle of a fine June night? I inched the drapes aside and peeked out the window. Not nearly dark; the sun was still above the roof of the north-south wing of the motel. I tossed my take-out wrappings into the wastebasket and opened *Science Digest*.

Who needed Chelon mad at him? Not me.

I flipped on the TV after a while, but the Twins had a travel day and there was nothing on I wanted to watch. Time stumbled on, leaning on its scythe for support.

At ten-thirty I turned off the news, picked up my junk, and went out to my car. This, too, was Chelon's idea, to leave early, in case my "friend"—why should I have such a friend?—decided to ambush me. I was also to keep an eye out, whatever that meant.

It meant a species of paranoia, I decided. I shivered slightly when a van pulled out from the curb behind me as I made a right turn onto Excelsior. Probably an unmarked escort, I comforted myself: Chelon hadn't said what he'd be driving. I moseyed on, and the van seemed to drop back a bit. Tactics?

Other than a bar, there's nowhere to go on that stretch of Excelsior at that time of a weeknight. The drugstore in the Miracle Mile was closing, so I couldn't even browse in the housewares aisle; the rest of the stores were dark or dimly lit, except for the restaurant. Minneapolis on a Tuesday is not a go-all-night town, and the suburbs are no livelier.

I pulled into the lot at Methodist Hospital, good and close to the building, and turned on the car radio to wait. I found a program featuring old opera records and listened to Amelita Galli-Curci warble, but it did nothing for my nerves. When a tall, fair guy strolled up to my car I almost caught his moustache in the window before I saw that it was Mack Forrester.

"How's it going?"

"Fine," I said. "Except I forgot the Kleenex to wipe my sweaty palms."

"Long as you haven't peed your pants."

"Not yet." I wasn't offering any guarantees. "Are you my escort?"

"Yeah."

"Was that you in the van, then?"

"What van?"

"Nothing, I guess. It pulled away from the curb when I came out of the motel drive, followed me."

"Get a look at the driver?"

"At this time of night? You've got to be kidding."

Mack shifted his stance, still leaning on the edge of my window, and looked around. "I don't see too many vans in the lot. What color?"

"Dark."

"I'll have a look around. Stay cool, J. J."

"Oh, sure."

A big, nearly full moon was coming up out of the northeast, and the insects in the marshy area west of the hospital were singing away. I closed my window against the mosquitoes that had zeroed in on me, slapped a couple, and spent the next few minutes listening to Galli-Curci with a whining accompaniment from the ones that remained.

Five till eleven, according to Texas Instruments. I took off my shirt, put on the bulletproof vest, replaced the shirt, and started the car. My hands slipped on the wheel as I backed out of the spot. *Breathe, breathe,* I told myself. *Just like Karen learned to do with the baby.*

I got to the light at the entrance, waited for it to turn green, and turned right. The light at Louisiana was green. One more short block. Behind me, Mack put his hand close to the Honda's windshield and gave me a thumbs-up sign.

North on Meadowbrook. I pulled into a no-parking zone, pretty sure I wouldn't get a ticket, and killed the engine. Bad verb. I turned it off. The Honda puttered past looking for a place of its own. I shut off my lights.

Two minutes till eleven.

I wondered where Chelon was. Everything looked perfectly normal, but that was the idea. Ahead of me, the taillights of the Honda turned left and disappeared around the bend that would eventually lead back to Excelsior. Place must be parked solid.

Which way would he come? Chelon guessed from the north, so I wouldn't be able to drive after him without turning around first on the narrow street. My heart hammered as if I'd jogged all the way around Lake Harriet *and* Lake Calhoun, and I was just as sweaty. Under the bulletproof vest, I started to itch.

There he was. Chelon had been right. I glanced at my watch. Only three minutes late; Chelon had thought five.

The Rabbit pulled up next to a hydrant on the other side of the street. The guy left the engine running. I rolled my window down, flinching as I did. Not that the glass would be any protection at all, but my mind couldn't explain that to my body's satisfaction. A faint, sweet floral perfume floated into the car.

Nothing else happened for a couple of minutes. Then the Rabbit's door opened and the man straightened up beside it. I cleared my throat. "Put your hands in the air, so I can see what's in them," I called.

The hands went slowly up, spread, empty in the light of the streetlights. "Middle of the street, we said."

"Right."

I opened my own car door and put my left foot out. A brilliant light caught the guy in the ski mask. "What the hell!" he shouted. He dove back into the Rabbit and gunned it into a screeching right turn onto Excelsior.

Headlights came on up the block. At the same moment, an engine revved nearer Excelsior. The bright light went out. "Hey, wait for me!" somebody shouted.

The unmarked police car coming south slowed fractionally

as the dark van swung into its path. The wheels turned right, the van hit the left rear fender, and the car spun and smashed into a parked car. Metal screamed.

Two engines cut off, one after the other. An instant of stunned silence, and then everyone started shouting at once.

The taillights of the Rabbit were long gone toward Hopkins. I sank back into my seat and did the breathing bit again before getting out of the car to join the people coming out of their apartments to see what all the excitement was about.

Chelon was dancing with anger, shaking a fist at a tall, willowy young man with curly hair. I'd seen that face with the perfectly cleft chin before, on Channel 7 News: Hugbetter. "Get that goddamn camera out of here before I chuck it in the creek!" Chelon shouted.

Hugbetter yelled something about a free press. Chelon offered him a free press under the wheels of the van, then whirled to give a series of instructions to a cop in uniform. I went over to the smashed unmarked car.

The driver was leaning against the steering wheel, his face resting on his arms. As I came up to the window, he lifted his head, and I saw that it was the black policeman I'd met before. A little blood dribbled out of his nose, a ghastly color in the blue streetlight. He wiped it away and looked at it on his fingers. "I blew it," he said, without looking up. "Sorry."

It was something, at least, to know that he could talk.

I stood around feeling useless while Chelon got people, instructions, and vehicles sorted out. The apartment dwellers lost interest and began to straggle back to their television screens, hurried along by the whining bugs. Only two or three diehards were left by the time the second tow truck came.

Chelon stood watching them string up the carcass of the van for a couple of minutes. Then he came over to me.

"See a license on that Rabbit?"

I shook my head. "It didn't have any plates."

"That's what it looked like from behind my bush, but I couldn't be sure." Chelon put his hands on his hips and watched the van groaning away on the hook of the tow truck. "Damn Hugbetter.

I'd take him in, but nothing sticks to these turkeys. Smoothed down by too many lawyers." He swore softly. "I've got my guys checking every tan Rabbit they see. The plates are back on it by now, I'll bet you anything. And it's probably parked in some garage."

"He had a different ski mask."

Chelon scratched at a bite on his bare forearm. "Yeah. He dropped the other one on an access road at the zoo. We found a couple of blond hairs in it. That's how I knew you hadn't faked it."

"Faked what?"

"That business at the zoo. You know, tossed your calling cards over the fence, draped yourself on the guard rail, and told a tall tale."

So much for the innate and shining honesty of my face. I shook my head, speechless.

"I sure wish I knew how he got past my guy at the other end of the street," Chelon said. "Let's go clean out that motel room. These bugs are murder tonight."

"Yeah." I started to get into the Ford. "Wait a minute," I said. "Where did he get another ski mask in June?"

Chelon was already walking away. "Maybe he knits," he said over his shoulder. He got into his car and slammed the door.

I slammed the door of my own, turned the key, and headed back to the motel. I didn't really care if I never saw the place again. Duty, as Ogden Nash once complained, hath not the visage of a sweetie or a cutie.

# XVI

Tired as I was, I went to work the next morning. Just to show you how unreliable omens can be, I found a spot in the unrestricted lot without any trouble at all. It was a real wrench to open the door of the Ford and get out, but I did it. And then I put one foot in front of the other and pointed myself at the entrance.

"Jamison!"

I turned toward the shout and got the sun in my eyes. A sour flutter of fear rose in my throat, and I made quickly for the heavy concrete pillars that support the portico of the building.

A hand on my elbow pulled me back, and Justin Hugbetter shoved a microphone at me. "Mr. Jamison," he said crisply, his newsman's voice. "Last night you were involved in a police raid. Care to tell us about it?"

"No," I said, scuttling sideways for the door. People were slowing as they walked past, with curious glances for the impeccably suited Hugbetter and the scruffy man with the TV camera on his shoulder.

"Would it have anything to do with the fact that you are living in a motel room?"

"None of your damn business, Hugbetter," I said.

"Would you be living in that motel room because of the recent fire that destroyed a portion of your home?"

"None of your business," I repeated. I tried to edge around him into the entrance, but he kept pushing the mike into my face.

"Your wife just had a baby, didn't she, Mr. Jamison?"

"Get out of my way."

Somebody was holding the door open for me. "She's not at home, and she wasn't with you at the motel," Hugbetter declared. "Where is she, Mr. Jamison?"

"None of your business," I said, squirting past him and into the lobby. Hugbetter followed. The security guard stood up behind his desk.

"Hey, you, where do you think you're going?" the guard demanded.

"I'm a guest of Mr. Jamison," Hugbetter said. The microphone had vanished.

"Throw him out," I told the guard.

"I want answers, Jamison," Hugbetter said. The guard had picked up his phone and punched four buttons. I helped out by standing still until two other guards appeared. Hugbetter went backward out the door, still protesting.

There are definite advantages to working for a company that has a few defense contracts, I decided. I scooted down the hall and up the back stairs to my own office and flopped into my chair.

"Another chapter?" Pedersen asked.

"Later," I said. "Right now, I need some coffee."

Pedersen grinned and took out a quarter, which he flipped. "Tails," I said.

He uncovered the coin. "Heads."


When I got back to my desk with the coffee, I found the first of a long series of curious visitors sitting in my chair, questioning Pedersen about the incident with Channel 7 at the entrance. After a few minutes, I was even invited to give my own version.

Pedersen had everyone pretty well briefed, it turned out. Not only that, but he'd established a whole network of spies. One of them came by with the news that Hudson's wife had filed for divorce on the Tuesday before Amant was killed.

"Indeed?" Pedersen's eyebrows climbed. "Interesting, don't you think, Jamison? That a woman would divorce a man on the brink of collecting a substantial inheritance from his recently deceased Aunt Charlotte?" He nodded without waiting for my opinion. "Yes. Another clue."

To my astonishment, he turned to the terminal on his desk and typed something in.

"What in hell are you doing?" I asked.

"Merely applying modern methods to solving this mystery," he explained. "Everything I have learned so far, I have stored in the computer. It remains only for me to complete my Sherlock Holmes program—"

"Pedersen, you're crazy. No computer is going to figure out who done it. Are you really sitting there collecting your salary for that?"

"Who did it," Pedersen corrected. "And you're not doing any more work than I am, so you're in no position to sniff and sneer."

"What kind of program are you writing, to sort all that stuff out?" I asked, interested in spite of myself. Hudson's Aunt Charlotte was presumably ensconced in the data base. The thought amused me. I wondered what Pedersen's program would make of marginal notes on Xerox copies.

"Medical-diagnosis programs have been in use for some time," Pedersen said. "And someone has a program for a psychological-screening interview. So it shouldn't be hard to adapt one of those diagnostic programs to evaluate motive, opportunity, and so forth."

"But..."

I had been going to point out the frequent inferiority of the Weather Service forecast programs to a wet finger held in the air, but I decided there was no point in arguing. Pedersen would do as Pedersen pleased, and he was right about the amount of work I was getting done. And as the day went on my productivity didn't improve any. I think I'd accomplished all of two hours' worth by the time the general going-home stir began. I joined the stir with no remorse.

I was half-afraid Hugbetter would be back at the door, but he'd apparently given up. I let a minute portion of the day's accumulated heat out of my car while I checked under the hood and looked at the pavement beneath it. Nothing wrong that I could see, so I went ahead and scorched my ass on the upholstery and headed for home.

Karen and Mrs. Eskew had prepared what the old lady called "a cold collation." It consisted of an extravagant amount of sliced meat and salad, set out elegantly on the screened back porch.

"I tried to stop her," Karen said helplessly.

"Nonsense," Mrs. Eskew said. "You've got to get your strength back after your ordeals, both of you. So sit down and eat and be happy."

I sat down at the table with the feeling that it had been a good six weeks since I'd awakened with the tigers, so all this was rather silly. But the food was delicious, and the three of us, with Joey in the bassinet beside us making little sucking noises and staring at a mobile that had sprouted from the porch ceiling while I was away, put most of the food where it would do our waistlines the least good.

"I had another run-in with the news media today," I remarked over dessert.

"Oh, no." Karen made a face at her raspberry sherbet. "What happened?"

"Hugbetter from Channel 7 met me at the door of the plant and asked about a million questions, none of which I answered. He seems to think somebody made off with you and Joey, since he doesn't know where you are."

Mrs. Eskew shuddered. "What a dreadful idea!"

"Oh, so that's what that was all about," Karen said thoughtfully. "I couldn't imagine what those people were doing. Then I thought, maybe it was something new they're doing for the insurance company."

"What are you talking about?"

"Oh, I went out on the porch this afternoon to see how the carpenters were doing, and I saw this guy standing in front of our house and somebody else with a TV camera taking his picture. So I went back in to ask Mrs. Eskew if anyone had said anything about taking pictures to her, but when we came out again to ask what was going on, the van was just pulling away from the curb."

"Where were the carpenters?"

"Sitting in the backyard, eating lunch."

"What did the guy look like? The one in front of the camera?"

"Oh, a light tan suit, bright brown hair with curls, very spiffy."

"Hugbetter. I wonder what he was up to?"

"Did you say Channel 7?" Mrs. Eskew asked. "It's only just six. Let's watch the news."

We trooped into the house, and she turned on the little black-

and-white portable she keeps in the kitchen. The glossy blonde anchorwoman told us urbanely about a subway train pileup somewhere in Europe, a couple of farm accidents, rumors of kickbacks in county government, and assorted other good news. The special report from investigative reporter Justin Hugbetter didn't come until after the first commercial break, in which KRAT-as-in-television-TV had managed to schedule ads for Treflan, Eradicane, *and* Lasso, just to stay even-handed on the herbicides, I guess, and finished up with a blurb for the alfalfa cows like best. I almost missed the first golden words, since not seeing a beer commercial reminded me that Mrs. Eskew had laid in a case of Blatz.

First, Hugbetter showed a carefully edited version of his "interview" with me. "None of your business," became "no." The pronunciation was a little odd, and the perceptive viewer might have wondered a bit, but so what? Hugbetter's handsome face filled the screen most of the time. There was a closeup of my own face as I scuttled through the door into the plant, though, and I was shocked at how old and tired I looked. I must have made some sound, because Karen reached across the kitchen table and squeezed my hand.

I took a long swig of beer.

Then the scene shifted to the front of our house. They must have been there a while before Karen spotted them, because Hugbetter went around to the side of the house and stirred some of the burnt straw, still there although scattered by carpenters and rain, with his immaculate hand. He prattled a bit about how the fire had been set.

Then he went on about my hospital admission. "Hospital authorities declined to comment, but Channel 7 News has learned from a reliable source"—Hugbetter smiled, the kind of smile you want to put a fist into—"that Mr. Jamison had suffered a head injury and was held for observation. But that was all of two days *after* the fire. How accident-prone can one man be?"

"I'd like to show him," I muttered. Karen patted my hand. "I wonder if I can get him for trespassing?"

"Then, too," Hugbetter continued, "hospital reports show that *Mrs.* Jamison gave birth to a boy, the day after the fire destroyed this bedroom in which she may have been sleeping. Shock? Perhaps. But it is interesting that she and her newborn son seem to have totally disappeared. Her husband is living all by himself in a motel room. Can it be that Mrs. Jamison and her young son have been abducted by the murderer of Victor Amant, whose body Mr. Jamison discovered just last week?"

Karen's breath hissed in. "How could he?" she gasped.

"Look!" Mrs. Eskew pointed at the television. In the background, behind Justin Hugbetter's chestnut curls but still in recognizable focus, Karen came onto Mrs. Eskew's porch. In her arms she held Joey. She watched for a moment as Hugbetter went into his windup, then went back through the door into the house. The old-fashioned screen door slammed behind her, obviously unlocked.

"He might as well have put up a billboard," Karen exclaimed bitterly.

My beer was empty; I wasn't sure how.

"...had to do with this police operation, which took place last night and in which the Channel 7 News team played an important role," Hugbetter said. My jaw sagged. The scene shifted: a man in a ski mask hurtled into a tan Volkswagen Rabbit and sped around a corner and away. Two other vehicles approached the intersection. The scene cut off before they collided: Hugbetter sat next to the glossy blonde in the studio, not a hair out of place. "If you have seen this car without license plates," he said, "or if you have seen someone putting license plates on a tan Volkswagen Rabbit, you should notify the St. Louis Park police department immediately." Hugbetter showed his perfect teeth. KRAT-TV engineers superimposed a telephone number over them, unreadable in black and white.

"Thank you, Justin," said the blonde.

The phone rang.

"It's for you," Mrs. Eskew said, holding it out to me. Just as well. I might have put my fist through her TV screen in another second or two.

"Hello?" I said.

"J. J., it's Mack. Did you see the news on Channel 7 just now?"

"I sure did."

"Listen, get Karen and the kid out of that house, check? And the old lady, too. Because if the killer saw that, you're in big trouble."

"I know it. Listen, Mack. I think we'll just go home. They finished putting up the Sheetrock today, so the dust is starting to settle."

"What about lights?"

"I can black them out. No problem."

Karen looked up and nodded. Out on the porch, Joey began crying, just as if he knew what was waiting for him at home.

"He's hungry," Karen said, getting up. I hung up and started to explain the plan to Mrs. Eskew.

"Oh, no," the old lady said. "Nobody's going to drive me out of my own house. I've lived here longer than your house has even existed, and I'm staying. You three can go next door, if you want. I'll be fine right here."

*Three?* I thought. Three. I was going to have to learn to count the baby. "What if this guy comes looking for one of us?" I asked. "He's already killed three people."

"He'll just have to deal with me."

The idea struck me as so ridiculous, I didn't know what to say. Mrs. Eskew sat in her dainty kitchen chair, looking straight back at me. She stood maybe five feet tall when drawn up to her full height in righteous indignation, and if she weighed in at ninety pounds, even after one of her cold collations, I'd be surprised. But there she was, as immovable as Gibraltar in her pastel plaid housedress.

"Mrs. Eskew..." I floundered.

"I have my pistol," she said, "and I know how to use it. So you don't have to worry about me."

"I could carry you over there," I said.

"Don't even try."

The argument continued until Joey had fallen into a sated sleep. In the end I was no match for a little old lady who had all the flexibility of a locomotive.

We sneaked into our own house through the backyard, like a pair of thieves in the night, except that it wasn't night yet. I put up the thermal shutters we use in the winter, so we could turn

[148]

on a couple of lights when it did get dark, and we settled in. The house was stuffy and airless, and all the heat of the day seemed to have concentrated in our family room. Joey lay quietly on his tummy in the bassinette, his little face beaded with sweat.

"Maybe we would be better off in a motel," I said.

"Joe, half your paycheck is going for motel bills this time," Karen protested. "We can stand one night here."

I looked at Joey. "But can he? And how do we know it will be only one night?" I had a sudden, panicky vision of living in fear the rest of our lives. Move to California, maybe, or Texas, one computer man in a crowd...

"Once we turn the lights out, we can take the shutters off a couple of windows," Karen said. "And as for more nights, or days, let's face that tomorrow."

I put an arm around her and nuzzled her hair. "Turning out the lights right now might not be such a bad idea," I murmured.

"Except that I'm still full of stitches," she said, pulling away. She faced me and smiled. "Soon."

"That's a promise."

We watched the ten-o'clock news on the color TV Mrs. Eskew had insisted on lending us, the sound so low it was almost inaudible. Not only did Hugbetter repeat his report, but he took pains to point out afterward that some viewers had called to ask if the woman and baby in the background might not be the missing Mrs. Jamison and her son.

Karen leaned forward without a word and twisted a knob, giving Hugbetter a bad case of jaundice.

"We don't know," he said, smiling into the camera as if he were about to launch into an ad for whiter, brighter teeth. "Mrs. Roland Eskew, who lives in that house, maintains that the woman is not Mrs. Jamison, but a niece who had brought her new daughter to visit. On the other hand, we made a photograph of that portion of our videotape and showed it to Mrs. Celia Dixon, who lives next door to the Jamison family on the other side. And she says that it *is* Mrs. Jamison."

Brief picture of Celia, in gardening gloves and hat, handing a large print back to Hugbetter and saying, "Yes, that's Karen." Her mouth formed the word *why?* but the sound had been cut.

"Oh, Celia," I groaned.

"Joe, you know what?" Karen said. "I just realized—We must have been right here in the house when he was out there talking to Celia." She giggled.

"He's lucky I didn't spot him," I said darkly. "I'd have run next door to borrow Mrs. Eskew's pistol and shot him right through his measly heart."

"I don't think he has one," Karen sighed. She readjusted the color and turned the TV off. "Let's not worry about it. Let's just get those shutters down, okay? I'm melting."

We turned out the lights, and I groped my way to one of the back windows. Somehow, I managed to get the shutters off and cross the room to take a set off the kitchen for cross-ventilation without breaking my neck or falling over the bassinet. I pulled out the knobs that keep the windows from opening more than a few inches, and opened them the few inches they would go. Joey stirred and made a little sound.

"I wonder if he'd rather be on his back," Karen whispered. "I wish I knew better what to do for him. He's so helpless, it scares me."

I felt pretty helpless myself, and it scared me, too.

I lay awake a long time, how long I didn't know. We have a clock that strikes the hours, on the mantel in the living room, but no one had been home to wind it when it ran down, and it was silent. I missed the tick.

Finally, I got up and shuffled into the kitchen to get myself a glass of water. I was standing at the sink, in the dark, looking out at the backyard, when I heard the shot.

A man screamed. A door banged.

Someone ran heavily through our yard and down the driveway, panting as if he had been running a long time. I tried to dash through the house to see where he went, but the shutters were still on the front windows and I couldn't get one down fast enough. A car was turning at the end of the block by the time I could put my face to the glass to look.

It didn't look like a tan Rabbit. Or any other color of Rabbit, for that matter.

Somebody tapped on our back door. I stumbled through the house toward the sound.

"What's going on?" Karen asked.

"I don't know."

"It's Lydia Eskew," said the person at the door. "May I come in?"

I opened the door as the light came on in the family room, and Mrs. Eskew bobbed through. "I got him! I know I got him!" she said gleefully. "I tried to phone you, but they're still putting you through to the motel."

"Who?" Karen demanded. "Got who?" She came to the kitchen door and put on another light.

"The man. He tried to get into my kitchen, and I just aimed like this—"

Horrified, I realized she had the pistol in her hands.

"—and fired!"

*Blam!*

A large hole appeared in the screen door. "Oh, dear," Mrs. Eskew said. "I guess I got carried away. Now all the mosquitoes will get in. And I've waked the baby."

Joey was indeed awake, and howling. Karen clung to the doorframe, staring at Mrs. Eskew.

"Uh, could you put the gun down, Mrs. Eskew?" I asked politely. "I don't think we'll be needing it for a few minutes."

She wrinkled her nose at the smell the shot had left in the room and put the pistol—it was a Luger, a souvenir of World War II, somebody told me later—on the kitchen table. "We'd better call the police," she said briskly, and went to the wall phone and dialed in a calm, businesslike manner that left me shaking. Well, at least the phone worked now for outgoing calls. I sat down at the table and stared at the pistol.

"This is almost too much," I told Karen.

"They'll be here right away," Mrs. Eskew reported cheerfully. "I wonder if I hurt him badly." She took the flashlight off the side of the refrigerator and shined it into the back yard. "I don't see much blood." She sounded disappointed.

I, who not so long before would not have cared if I had never seen another man in blue in my life, could hardly wait for the police to arrive.

And what with the recent city budget cutbacks, it took them an eternity. Long enough for me to put on my pants and sit down again. Four minutes, at a guess.

Karen and I sat in exhausted silence, too tired even to climb back onto the bare mattress of the hide-a-bed. Joey was asleep again, the deep sleep of infancy, and the police had followed Mrs. Eskew over to her house and had eventually gone away.

"I can't take much more of this, Joe," Karen said. "I'm even thinking of visiting Mom and Dad in Florida."

"I'm not sure how much more I can take myself," I said.

"I thought you'd catch that guy last night," Karen sighed. "I really thought you would."

"So did I."

"That damned reporter. Why couldn't he keep his perfect nose out of our business?"

"I didn't think that much of his nose myself."

"Oh!"

"Karen," I said, "douse that light."

"Why?" She leaned out of the chair and reached for the lamp. I got up and hit the switch in the kitchen and checked the back-door lock and put up the chain.

"I just remembered something," I explained. "We aren't out of the woods yet. That was the wrong car out there."

"What are you talking about?"

"The car that drove away from Mrs. Eskew's shooting match. Our guy drives a Rabbit. That was a big car, a Mercedes maybe."

"A Mercedes!" Karen shifted in the darkness. "I thought you meant this was an ordinary burglar. What kind of burglar drives a Mercedes?"

"I've heard of it," I said defensively. "There was that guy in Duluth, had a couple of houses and a bunch of fancy cars...."

"But he robbed rich people, not people in a neighborhood like this. Now, if—"

"Karen! Keep your voice down."

She stopped talking entirely and went to the front window

[152]

to look out, walking confidently through the dark. The moon had turned the sheer curtains white, and she looked very slender against them, her face and shoulder rimmed with light.

"No one out there," she said softly. I got up again and went to the kitchen window. The backyard was well lit, moonlight away from the house and the Dixon's yard light filling in the shadows nearer. I could see nothing lurking in the yard but the bird feeder.

"No one here, either," I reported.

"Let's go back to bed." She came back through the darkened house, holding on to the furniture. I could see her shadow pause, hear her tired shuffle.

"Are you all right?" I asked.

She sank onto the edge of the mattress opposite me and lay down slowly. "Just very, very tired."

I tossed my pants onto the back of the recliner and lay down myself, smiling as my spine adjusted to the horizontal surface. One of the great pleasures of life, to lie on something firm and soft, when your body has gone as far as it can go, and close your eyes.

Outdoors, a car door closed with a solid thunk. I heard quick footsteps going up the sidewalk. Somebody else's problem, I thought. About time for it to be somebody else's problem.

A couple of minutes later, the footsteps ran back toward our house. I heard them thud across the lawn, and then someone pounded on our front door. "J. J.," called a woman's voice. "J. J., are you in there?"

I got my muscles together and hauled myself upright. "Just a minute," I yelled. Beside me, Karen murmured sleepily.

I reached the door and leaned against it. "Who is it?" I asked wearily.

"Anne Streich. Can I come in?"

I undid the lock and opened the door a crack. She pushed herself into the crack, slid into the house, and leaned the door shut behind her. "Where are you?" she whispered. "I can't see anything."

A click in the family room, and some yellow light spilled over us. "What's going on?" Karen called.

[153]

"It's Anne Streich," I said. I started toward the light, painfully aware that I was wearing only my boxer shorts and was none too sure that it wasn't one of the pairs with the seat worn gauze thin. "Just let me get my pants on, will you, Mrs. Streich?" I asked.

"Anne," she said, right behind me. I snatched my jeans from the back of the recliner and stood behind it to pull them on.

Karen was sitting on the bare mattress in her nightgown with her legs out straight in front of her, looking very young. She stared first at me and then at Anne Streich.

"I called," Anne said. "And I got that phone company recording that said to call you at the motel, but you weren't in that room any more, so I came over to see if you were with that woman who was on the news after all, and you weren't there, and oh, I'm so glad I've found you!" She wrung her hands together so tightly that I thought her fingers might come off. Karen's mouth fell open.

"What's the matter?" I asked. I sat down on the recliner and brushed the hair out of my eyes. My mouth felt like the inside of an old well.

"It's Harry," Anne said. "He's been shot."

# XVII

THERE comes a point at which there is no emotion left, and I had reached it. I sat on the edge of the recliner with my forearms on my knees and looked at Anne Streich without reaction.

"Didn't you hear me?" She plunked down on the mattress next to Karen and reached out with both hands. "Harry's been shot. He came home covered with blood. He says it was somebody trying to mug him, but I didn't hear any shot, and I'm *sure* it must have been this same man who killed David."

Joey started to cry.

The effect on Anne Streich was astonishing. She jumped up and went over to the bassinet and picked my son up and started to rock him against her shoulder. Karen stared. Anne murmured and cooed at the baby until he stopped crying, and then she laid him very gently back in the bassinet and turned to Karen. "You really should have some help," she said. "It's very tiring, these first few weeks as a new mother."

"But...your husband?" Karen said. She sounded puzzled.

Anne put her face in her hands. "I'm so tired," she mumbled. "I can't think straight."

"Where's Harry now?" I asked. I had to repeat the question twice before Anne lifted her head and looked at me.

"He's at Methodist. I drove him over.... Oh, the car's got blood all over it...." She swallowed. "He says he has to see you right away. He won't say what it's about."

Karen looked at me. "I guess you'll have to go."

"What will I do about you?" I protested. "I can't leave you alone here, not after that news report. And I'm not so sure I want you back next door with Mrs. Eskew and her pistol, either."

"We'll stay here," Karen said. Her voice trembled. "I'll be fine. I just want to get this over with."

"So do I," Anne said. "Ever since Paula died, it seems like everything's coming apart."

"Go," Karen said to me. "See what happened. Maybe we can get it all cleared up and get on with our lives."

I shook my head.

[ 155 ]

"I'll call up the Dixons and explain, ask them to put me and Joey up for the rest of the night. Please, Joe, just go and get it over with."

I looked at the two women sitting in the light of the one lamp, my wife with a worried, half-hopeful expression, Anne Streich staring at her lap, her forehead creased. I sighed. "All right," I conceded. "I'm too tired to argue. Just let me get a shirt on, and some shoes."

I did that, escorted Karen and Joey across the driveways to the Dixons', and took the car keys Anne held out to me. For the first time in my life, I had the chance to drive a real luxury car. Unfortunately, I was in no condition to appreciate the opportunity. Just glad to get the damned thing parked without any dents.

Harry Streich was still in surgery when we got to the hospital. He'd been shot in the left thigh with a large-caliber weapon. Quite a lot of blood lost, the surgeon informed us an hour or so later, and some delicate repairs to be made to nerves and blood vessels, but no major lasting damage to be expected. No, we couldn't see him.

"But Harry asked to see J. J.," Anne pleaded. "He insisted, no one but J. J."

The surgeon glanced at me as if wondering what sort of magician I might be. "He's still under the anaesthetic, Mrs. Streich," he explained. "He can't talk to anybody."

I was more than half-asleep, and just as happy. "Maybe I should go home," I said. "Come back when he's in better condition."

"I think that's a fine—" the surgeon began.

"No!" Anne interrupted. "The instant he's awake, J. J. goes to talk to him. It has to be important, or Harry wouldn't have asked."

I have heard people describe their minds as being in ferment. I wouldn't exactly say that about my own at that moment, but a couple of bubbles rolled lazily to the surface and popped. "How's he been lately?" I asked. "Ready to talk to you about David yet?"

The surgeon slipped out of the room. Anne's eyes followed

[156]

him, and her mouth set in a bitter line. "Not to me. He goes over to Ben's and gets plastered, but he won't talk to his own wife."

"Is that where he was this evening?"

"I told you, I don't believe that story."

"Well, but was he at Ben's house?"

"There, or out in a bar, or somewhere with him."

I noticed, in a dull sort of way, that Anne Streich without makeup, wearing mismatched shirt and shorts and dirty rubber thongs, didn't look as out of place on the turquoise plastic upholstery as I might have expected. She looked, in fact, like a middle-aged woman who had had too much sun and not enough to do for years, and the crooked smile now looked more like habit than interest. "I never liked Ben anyway, if you want to know."

I didn't, but I let her talk.

"Harry…" She was back to her husband. I pushed my hands a little deeper into my pockets and rested the back of my neck on the sticky vinyl back of the chair I was sitting in and hoped I wouldn't snore if I dropped off.

"Harry is deep," Anne said. "You don't know, because he hides it with all his bluff and practical jokes, but he has *feeling*. Ben, now." She sighed heavily. "I don't know about Ben. Sometimes I think he married Paula for her money and was just as glad when she drank herself to death."

Another little bubble rose to the surface of my mind and burst. "Excuse me a minute," I said. "I have to use the men's room." She made a disappointed little *moue* and flounced back in her chair.

I thought I'd seen a pay phone in the hall, and I had. I even found some change in my pocket, enough to dial the police station in St. Louis Park. I asked for Richard Chelon and lucked out—he was on duty.

He came on the line almost instantly. "Jamison? What kind of jam are you in now?"

"Listen. I'm at Methodist. You might be interested to know that Harry Streich—that's the father of the boy who was killed, the one who built the saucer—has been shot and is just out of surgery."

[157]

"Is he?" Chelon said. "You're right. That is interesting. I might just drop by."

"If you do, bring that envelope."

I hung up before he could ask any more questions or Anne could come wandering out into the hall, and returned to the lounge where the surgeon comes to talk to the waiting relations. Anne was asleep, snoring unglamorously against the back of the chair.

A few minutes later, after I had explored all I wanted of a tattered issue of *Time* and was poking around for something else to read, a nurse came into the room and asked if one of us were J. J. Jamison. I owned up.

"Harry Streich is awake and asking for you," she said.

I nodded toward Anne. "That's his wife."

The nurse glanced at her. "You go on up," she said, handing me a card with the room number on it. "I'll wake her up and send her after you."

I went out to the elevators and punched the up button. Would I meet the mad doctor? I wondered. Pedersen had collected some more dirt on the guy — what, I couldn't remember. Pedersen could be a real menace if he wanted to be, I reflected. Make himself a mint, and all tax-free, selling his little bits of information.

The elevator opened, looking just as bleak as the hour of the night demanded. I stepped in and gave the floor button a poke. The doors hummed closed. I traveled upward without interruption and was deposited on Harry Streich's floor.

He was watching for me, and he almost tried to get out of bed.

"What is your evidence?" he asked, without even saying hello. He was thick tongued with anesthesia but still forceful. A mean man at a board meeting, I thought.

"Evidence of what?"

"The evidence you have against my son."

Was that what was of such burning importance? I looked over at the other bed in the room. It was empty. I wondered how long the police would buy whatever he had told them. I pulled the chair over and sat down. "His friend Bob Evans helped him build the saucer," I said. "He was quite proud of it, in fact, and I can understand why. A good job. And there are bits and pieces of physical evidence that link him to the saucer as well. But I wouldn't worry about it. A hoax like that doesn't seem too serious to me. It didn't get out of hand, like the other one."

Streich made an impatient gesture. "Not the saucer," he said. "I don't give a damn about that. What's the evidence you have connecting my son with this Victor Amant?"

"With Victor Amant?" I gaped at him. "None."

"None? Is that true?"

"Absolutely. I don't think he had the faintest idea that Victor Amant even existed."

Streich relaxed against the pillow. "I've made some terrible mistakes," he said.

I waited.

"And I almost made another one. I was going to take your boy." He stopped and looked at me.

"Take my son? You? Why?"

"To hold. Against your giving me the evidence. Ben said you had an envelope—"

Anne appeared timidly at the door to the room. "Can I come in?" she asked.

"Please," Harry said. She went up to him, on the other side of the bed, and kissed his forehead. "Sit down, dear," he ordered.

She looked around, saw no other chair, and perched on the edge of the bed. Her husband smiled at her. "I've been saved from something I don't quite understand," he said. "I guess it's a good thing that old lady took a shot at me."

"Old lady? An old lady tried to mug you?"

"Well..." Harry Streich sighed. "No. Not exactly."

"What did happen, then?"

"Did you see the news on Channel 7 tonight?"

Anne glanced at me and back at her husband. "Yes. But what does that have to do with you?"

"I tried to kidnap the little boy."

"J. J.'s baby?" Anne goggled at him. "Harry, why?"

Harry Streich gazed into the distance and sighed deeply. "Ben told me there's some evidence that David arranged the murder of this Amant person."

"Harry, not possible! Why should David want to murder a perfect stranger?"

"Maybe he wasn't a perfect stranger," Streich said. "Maybe David knew him and thought he'd killed his aunt."

Someone else tapped at the door. "May I join this conversation?" Chelon asked. He walked in without waiting for an answer. Mack Forrester followed him in and shut the door. "You wanted this?" Chelon asked, extending the brown envelope.

I took it. "This is what Ben wanted," I told the Streichs. "Some pictures. A plastic bag. A Xerox of two pages in a book." I took the pictures and the Xerox out and spread them out on the bed. Anne recoiled.

"That's Lala!" she said. "Where did you get these? That's Lala, dead! Just the way I found her."

Chelon moved suddenly, but the Streichs paid no attention.

"Why…are these police pictures, is that it? You got these from the Edina police. Is that it?"

"No," I said. "I'm sorry. Look carefully."

"The gin bottle is in the picture," Anne said dully. "The one I took away and hid. Somebody must have taken these before I got there. And what's this spot by her face? That wasn't there when I found her."

"Look at the other pictures," I suggested. "See what you can tell me about them."

"It's Paula's kitchen," Anne said. "It must be that day. It was snowing…. What's happened to the kitchen counter? It was never like that."

Chelon leaned over and whispered something to Mack, who quietly slipped out the door.

"Look at the Xerox," I said.

"If a man wanted to commit the perfect murder, he should… carbon dioxide…" she read. "I don't quite see…Oh! Dry ice! But what…?"

She seemed to have drawn into herself as she passed the Xerox to her husband with a puzzled glance. He read it too, blinking hard every couple of seconds. "Oh…my…God!" he said. "I do see. Somebody put some dry ice next to her face and pulled the covers up—that's the spot, water that condensed on

[160]

the dry ice. And the kitchen counter—could dry ice have done that? Frozen it, so something happened to it? But who took the pictures?"

"I'm not sure," I said, "but I think it was Victor Amant."

Anne Streich stared at me. She had wrapped her arms tightly around her middle, and her face was a gray mask like her husband's. "Then that's who Toro was," she almost whispered. "Paula told me about him. Last winter. She met him in a bar, and she fell in love. Paula was always falling in love. I didn't pay much attention, until she said she was thinking about a divorce." She blinked twice. "Is that who killed her? Toro?"

Harry Streich shook his head.

"I don't think so," I said. "I think he just happened onto the scene and took the pictures. Maybe he was supposed to meet her and walked in on her dead. Then he figured he'd do a little blackmail."

"How...mercenary. But who killed her?"

"Her husband, I think," I said, as gently as I could.

"Ben?"

"Ben's just a practical joker," Harry said. "If he did kill Lala, it was an accident. Why would he want her dead?"

"Money?"

They both stared at me. I shrugged. "I can't be sure about it. But if he did, his fingerprints are most likely on the plastic sack in this envelope. I think it was the sack that held the dry ice. It's that fuzzy thing on the kitchen counter, the cold sack covered with frost."

Anne hurriedly gathered the photographs together and thrust them at me with a shudder. "This is too ghoulish," she said. "I can't take any more."

"Me, either," I said. "He's been after me for ten days now. It's getting so I can't see any color of Volkswagen Rabbit without flinching."

"Rabbit?" Anne's mouth slipped open. "But Ben doesn't drive a Rabbit. He drives a Toyota Celica. He bought it just last month."

A Toyota Celica. The car Amant had been found in. And the Illinois plates?

Mack caught my eye. "The Rabbit belonged to Amant. We just got the report from Illinois." Chelon slammed him into silence with a blink.

The cars had been switched? What sense did that make?

"Where's Gale now?" Chelon asked.

"Gale?" I asked.

"That's Ben's last name," Anne said. "He should be here. I called him and asked him to come, before I went and got J. J. That was a couple of hours ago."

At a glance from Chelon, Mack slipped out of the room. Harry Streich closed his eyes. "I'm very tired," he said. "If you don't mind, I'd like to be alone with my wife."

"Toro! Lala!" Chelon snorted, on the way down in the elevator. "These people walk around calling each other names I wouldn't paste on a toy poodle."

The elevator stopped on the next floor, and a weary-looking man got in. He leaned against the wall and the three of us eyed each other until the car reached the ground floor. Chelon and I walked out.

"Now, Ben Gale," Chelon sighed. "He's probably in a plane on his way to Brazil by now."

"He moves fast," I agreed. "He talked Streich into trying to kidnap my kid earlier tonight. When he heard about Streich getting shot, I bet he took off like a rocket."

"You shoot Streich?" Chelon asked.

"No, the old lady next door did."

"Some neighborhood you live in. Well, the big city. Where's your car?"

"Home. I'll catch a bus or walk."

Chelon paused outside the hospital entrance. "How come Harry Streich wanted your son?"

"He thought I had some evidence connecting David to the Amant murder. Gale got him drunk and fed him a line, I guess. So, since they'd seen that newscast and thought they knew where Joey was—"

"What newscast?"

"Channel 7. You didn't see it?"

[162]

"Missed it."

I summarized Hugbetter's latest effort, soft-pedaling the part about taking part in a police operation in deference to Chelon's cardiovascular system. An ambulance turned in from Excelsior Boulevard, cut the siren, and sped toward us. Chelon nodded at it.

"That Hugbetter," he said. "Maybe one of these days he'll get caught in the crossfire and do the world a favor."

"He could have a great career posing for the Sears catalog," I agreed. "Keep him out of mischief."

Chelon gave me a half salute, and I set off through the parking lot, which was almost as brightly lit by the moon as it was by the tall light standards with their clouds of suicidal moths. The reeds in the marshy area west of the lot whispered huskily, the katydids argued about whether Katy had or hadn't, a few nighthawks circled overhead with their penny-whistle cries. I was still quite a distance from where I had first seen that Toyota, half my life ago.

An outline of what might have happened began to shimmer in my head. Gale had killed his wife, Anne Streich's sister. Amant had found out, tried blackmail. How? Gale had agreed to pay him for the evidence, Amant had for one reason or another made the day's drive from Chicago, and Gale had met him and killed him. Maybe in his own car, uncleanable—was that why they'd been switched? Okay. The plates had been switched to delay discovery, and Gale had left the car in the lot. *With his nephew floating down the creek in a fake UFO. Sure, sure, Jamison. All planned ahead. Won't wash.*

And then there was Harry Streich. I hadn't been paying close enough attention to Harry Streich, I realized: too full of my own importance. Now, too late, I began to wonder about that scene a few minutes before. Had there been something a little ...what? Awkward? Play-acted?...about it?

The big greenish windows of an MTC bus zipped along Excelsior Boulevard and paused at the bus shelter long enough to let off a lone woman, who hurried toward the hospital with nervous glances behind her. Not a hope in a hundred that I could catch the bus: I thought of offering to walk back with the woman and decided it was a good way to get kicked in an uncomfortable place.

And then somebody took a shot at me.

A bullet going past your ear doesn't *krang* like it does in the movies. The sound is indescribable. But it produces an automatic reaction, even if you've never heard it before. You duck.

I lay on the asphalt beside a car. The woman was running toward the hospital, screaming at the top of her lungs. I wanted to tell her, *That's okay, lady, it's got nothing to do with you.* Instead, I lay still feeling the night turn cold.

Better to be on my feet.

I drew my legs up into a crouch and listened. The woman was making good time; she must be nearly to the building.

Gravel turned under a shoe.

Impossible to tell where. I squatted and balanced against the car with one hand. In the next line over I noticed a Jeepster I thought would make better cover than the little Chevette I was cowering against, and I decided to make a run for it, bent low the way they do on TV.

Mistake. He was between the rows, and another shot screamed over my head.

A car gunned toward us from the direction of the hospital. *Dear God*, I thought, *don't let him hit anybody. And get it past, get the damn car past—I can't hear where he is.*

The car screeched to a halt. "Gale?" Chelon shouted. "Come out with your hands up. This is the police."

I dodged around the Jeepster and raised my head to see if I could spot Gale through the windows. He was sauntering toward me, his fair hair gleaming in the moonlight. I ducked and tried to keep the wagon between us.

Another shot. Glass in the Jeepster splintered. And a second shot, almost instantly, but I was already running, crouched over, along the line of cars. In the far, far distance I heard a siren begin to wail. I fell flat and rolled under a van and waited, panting.

"Give up, Gale!" I heard Chelon yell. "You haven't got a chance."

"Come and get me!"

Someone ran toward me. I cringed under the van, but the

steps ran on past, headed for the creek a few yards upstream of where it vanished under the road. "The bridge!" I shouted. "Don't let him get away under the bridge!"

More running steps, as I tried to hitch out from under the van. A shriek. A splash.

The yelping siren turned in at the hospital drive. Brakes. More running.

I got myself out from under the van and started toward the creek. Someone ran up behind me and pinned my arms. "Move, and you're dead," he said. I held very still.

"Police?" I asked.

"Believe it, baby."

"Listen, the guy you want is in the creek." My throat was so dry I could hardly get the words out. "Don't let him get away under the bridge."

"Hey!" Chelon. "Give a hand, here. You can let go of that guy, McManus."

The cop who had hold of me was running almost before he let go. I staggered against the van and got my balance. The shooting seemed to have stopped. Cautiously, I went toward the group on the short grass beside the marsh.

"He's in there somewhere," Chelon was saying. "He's armed. McManus, get across the road and check out the other side of the bridge. Jamison, get out of here."

I retreated behind a couple of cars. The marsh was eerily silent, the one sound the alarm call of a single blackbird.

"Haul that spotlight over here," I heard Chelon order. One of the cops dashed past me, and a moment later the squad car drew up beside the edge of the parking lot. A bright light flashed into the marsh. "There he is. What in hell?"

Someone splashed into the muck. "He's tangled up in something. I can't tell— Oh, jeez, I think he's bought it."

"Wounded?"

"Give me a hand." The splashing increased. I ventured out from behind the cars and saw Chelon and one of the men dragging Ben Gale's limp body toward the grass. Chelon spotted me and waved me over. "Yell for McManus," he called. "Tell him we've got him."

"Coming," came a ghostly shout from the mouth of the bridge.

Someone held out a hand to Chelon and helped him up the bank as he dragged on Gale with his other hand. Different uniform on the legs showing in the reflected light. Someone from hospital security, I guessed.

"Get the light on him," Chelon demanded.

Even before the light was re-aimed, I could see that Gale wasn't breathing. His head dropped back, and with one of those flashes of insight that hits at the oddest moments, I thought: *Eileen. Ellie.* Linda was Benjamin Gale's girl!

"Oh, Christ," said Chelon. "I get to give this bastard the kiss of life."

By the time Gale had been revived and hospitalized and I had signed yet another statement for Sergeant Chelon, the sun had risen. Mack Forrester was going off duty, and I got a ride home after all.

# XVIII

I emptied the last sack of grass clippings and stashed the lawn-mower in the garage. Joey was asleep in his bassinet on the screened porch as I passed through. "Someday, my boy, this will all be yours," I promised him. "Especially the lawnmower."

"I told her to let you finish," said a familiar voice.

"Hi, Mack. Where's your beer?"

"I just got here." Mack was sprawled on my recliner, big, hairy blond legs stretched out in front of him. I hooked the caps off a couple of the case of Michelob I'd bought that morning and handed him one. He put about half of it down in one gulp and sighed noisily.

"We got a confession," he said. "Just like you thought. Gale killed his wife. Then Amant came along and started blackmailing him—"

"Hold on a minute," Karen interrupted, coming out of the kitchen with a bowl of potato chips. "I missed most of this, so you'll have to run through it again for me." She set the chips down on the coffee table and ate one.

"Let me," I said. "You can correct as I go along, right, Mack?"

"Show off." Mack held out his empty bottle.

I raised an eyebrow at it. "Show off yourself." I took the bottle and replaced it with a full one. "One thing I don't understand is what prompted the UFO business."

"Yes," Karen said. "That bothers me, too. It's so...*cute.*"

"The whole thing is cute," Mack said. "He says he got the idea because he saw an airplane that looked like a flying saucer. I don't know what he really saw, but that's what he says."

"Anyway," I said, "sometime late last winter, Gale decided to get rid of his wife. She was a drunk, she had a lot of money that would be his if she died, she wanted a divorce, and he had a girl-friend. Linda."

"Eileen," Mack corrected. He smiled at his bottle and took another gulp.

"I can keep this straighter if you let me call her Linda," I said.

"Suit yourself." Mack went back to his beer. I heard a curse from the bedroom, where a Sheetrock man was tramping around in stilts, slathering spackle on the ceiling.

"So one morning before she woke up, he fixed up some dry ice so that as it melted, or whatever it does, she'd suffocate. No marks on her, nothing to indicate anything wrong. Then he put a little gin in her mouth, so she'd smell as if she'd been drinking —or maybe she really had been drinking; I don't know."

Mack nodded. "Blood alcohol was right up there."

"He left the house, intending to tidy up later—throw out the rest of the dry ice, maybe put away the book, so on. Only what he didn't know was that Paula's boyfriend, Amant, was coming over. Plain bad luck, I guess."

Mack snorted. "Plain stupidity. She told him she was going away with Amant the night before—that's why she was drunk; they'd been arguing—and the yoyo never dreamed Amant would come to the house to pick her up. Thought she'd just go meet Amant somewhere, like he'd have a girl do himself. So he took what looked like his last chance." Mack shrugged. "Left the sack of dry ice open on the kitchen counter to get rid of it. Stuck the book on the hall table so he'd remember to take it back to the library."

Mack held out his empty bottle. Karen took it, gave the bowl of potato chips a suggestive little shove, and came back with another beer.

"Take it easy, Mack," I said. "I only got one case."

"Anyway," Karen prompted me.

"Anyway, Amant came for Paula, found her dead, took his pictures and the bag, saw the book, and took that. I don't know how he made the contact to start his blackmail. That's for you guys," I said to Mack, "when you're sober."

Mack lifted an eyebrow and balanced the bottle on his belly.

"But he did," I went on, "and Gale decided to get rid of him, too. So he cooked up this business so the UFO would look like a distraction and got his nephew, an old hand at hoaxing, to make him a UFO."

Karen frowned. "I thought Gale was in a restaurant with Anne

[ 168 ]

Streich when the UFO was sighted. How could he be killing Amant in the parking lot at the same time?"

"Ah!" I lifted a finger. "He didn't. That's exactly what he wanted people to think, and I fell for it all the way."

"If you'd ever asked what time the guy died, you might have learned something," Mack said.

"Not really. Between seven and midnight. It fits."

Mack shrugged.

"He arranged to meet Amant somewhere—"

"Parking ramp in Edina," Mack put in. "Amant did the arranging—he was on his way back from vacation, and he was dumb enough to give Gale a month's warning. Plenty of time to get his plan going."

"And Gale shot him," I continued. "Amant's wound was on the left side of his head, so his killer must have been to his left. In fact, Amant was sitting in the passenger seat of Gale's Toyota, and now Gale had blood all over his car. Disaster."

"Not really," Mack said. "That was part of the plan. He even took the serial numbers off the Celica."

"You're kidding!"

"Scout's honor," Mack said, draining his beer. "He had the gun under the edge of the seat. First he showed Amant that he didn't have a weapon—got out of the car, and so on—then he said he had the money in the glove compartment of the Celica. Suggested maybe Amant wouldn't want to be seen getting paid off. So Amant got into the Celica and opened the glove compartment at Gale's invitation, and Gale shoved his head down and shot him with the gun he'd picked up while Amant was looking for the money."

"He planned to switch the plates?"

Mack made a little side-to-side gesture with his free hand. "More cute. Thought it would confuse the issue—but he forgot to lift Amant's wallet."

"And here I thought he was just making a spur-of-the-moment recovery," I sighed. "Oh, well. Then he drove the Celica out to the hospital lot, parked it where he thought nobody would look at it too soon, walked out to Excelsior, hopped a bus—"

[169]

"Actually, he jogged to the Miracle Mile and took a cab," Mack said. "After wiping the Celica down."

"Wiping it down?" Karen asked.

"No fingerprints but Amant's."

I stopped to digest that. "I think he made a habit of wearing gloves," I said, remembering the gloves Gale had pulled off in the Streichs' kitchen. "Anyway, then he gave the envelope to Linda for safekeeping."

"Why would he want to save it?" Karen asked, handing Mack another beer.

"He didn't." Mack put the bottle on the table beside him without even drinking any. "He gave it to her to get rid of."

I sat blinking at him. "Oh," I picked up. "She decided to go him one better and pin the murder on me?"

Mack nodded.

"But why Joe?" Karen asked.

"He found the body. On TV, it's always the guy who finds the body who's suspected first," Mack explained. "But J. J. left something out. The first thing Amant did, before the blackmail, was to nick Gale's brake line, just like Gale did later to the Streich kid and to you. Scared hell out of Gale." Mack's eyes were closed; you wouldn't think he'd been talking. "Amant had some crazy idea of revenging himself on Gale. He took the pictures so he could throw himself on the mercy of the court, or something, if he got caught. Then he thought of blackmail, and he liked that better—or so he told Gale."

"So it was Gale's car that was tampered with," I mused. "No wonder Linda thought twice."

"Yeah. Well, go on. I'm enjoying this."

I gave Mack a suspicious glance, but he'd closed his eyes again. "Okay. So Linda gave me the evidence. She told Gale what she'd done, and he didn't like it—the evidence was out of his control."

"Not that it was much in the way of evidence," Mack commented.

"Guilty minds magnify," I explained. I'd caught more than one hoaxer for just that reason. "He thought it was bad enough. He

[170]

got her to make that call to me, and then he shot her and dumped her body."

"And the gun," Mack said. "We found that in the culvert."

"What was he shooting with last night?" Karen asked.

"Another one," Mack said. "You got the money, you can buy 'em like Hershey Bars."

"Then he came back here and set the fire," I continued, "thinking to get both me and the envelope. But we were at the hospital having a baby." It occurred to me that I had owed my son my life before he was even born.

"It must have been Gale who broke in and stole the TV," Karen said. "To cover looking for the envelope. Oh, brother! This is making my head hurt."

Mack leered at her.

"I forgot," I said. "Somewhere in there he went back to the parking ramp and picked up Amant's Rabbit."

"That's where he went with the cab," Mack supplied. "We found it on the cabbie's log sheet. Once you know what you're looking for, you'd be surprised what you find. Then he drove over to Linda–Eileen's and left the envelope off. She was in it from the beginning, by the way. Plus something else I'm going to wait to see if you mention. That's one reason he had to get rid of her when things started to snowball on him."

"And I thought she looked like such an innocent kid," I sighed. "Well. He didn't dare drive the Rabbit around too much, because somebody might see him who would know it wasn't his car."

"And besides," Mack added, "once somebody got the plate number, we'd know it belonged to Gale's Toyota, and that would be it."

"I never thought of that."

Mack grinned. "Take heart. It took our mastermind a couple of days too. I just thought I'd throw it in."

"But then he didn't have the Celica. So he said it was in for repairs."

"What about those other attacks on you?" Karen asked. "The brake line, and going after you on your bike?"

"He'd seen me with the Streichs at the funeral home, and again

[171]

at the funeral. He knew I knew that David had done that old hoax, the one that inspired his plan, and he was afraid I'd make the connection. So he was trying to scare me off."

Mack pointed the neck of his bottle at me. "You owe your life to a pothole, old buddy. Gale wasn't just playing games."

"And the fire?" Karen asked, after a moment in which the only sound was the tramp and click of the Sheetrocker's stilts.

"Maybe he figured we'd escape but the envelope would be burned?"

Mack gave me a sharp glance. "You got to stop thinking like a normal person. Don't let your heart bleed for Gale. He's one of those comes with no conscience. There was kerosene all over the place. If it had caught, bye-bye house."

"Oh," I said.

Mack grinned. "Cops talk to everybody. Even firemen and in-surance adjustors."

"What about David?" Karen asked. "How did he do that?"

"The pizza place is right next door to where he took Anne to dinner. He excused himself to go to the men's room, took a hack-saw to the MG's brake line for a second or two, met David as ar-ranged, paid him, went back to his table…"

Karen shuddered. "That's nerve. I'm sorry I asked."

"Oh, he had nerve. No doubt about that." Speaking of nerve, Mack got up and went out to the kitchen and came back with three open bottles of beer. He handed one to me and one to Karen and sat down to hold the recliner down some more.

"Not a reliable method, the brake line, as Mack pointed out," I said. "But if it didn't work, he'd get another chance before David learned about the body in the parking lot and got to think-ing. He lived a couple of blocks away, and he had a key to the Streichs' house. So he could have managed something, though it wouldn't have been as neat as the accident."

"He liked accidents," Mack mumbled.

Karen shook her head. "And the tigers?"

"Scare you dead," Mack suggested, grinning again.

"But drive way out to the zoo, just to throw somebody to the tigers, when he'd already shot two people?" Karen objected. "It doesn't sound like the rest."

Mack smiled at his new beer as if they shared a secret.

"Maybe Mrs. Eskew was right," I said. "He was letting fate decide. Anyhow, the rest you can figure out. He was watching the want ads to see if I tried to contact Linda, and Chelon's ad flushed him out. Hugbetter messed that up. But then Hugbetter put us back on track—inadvertently, of course."

"Poor Harry Streich," Karen said. "He can't have suspected what he had for a brother-in-law."

Mack smiled at his beer some more.

"Then, last night," I said, "Anne told Gale she was going to pick me up and bring me to the hospital. He saw another chance and waited for me in the lot. When Chelon showed up, he tried to get away down the creek, but he got stuck in the muck or something."

Mack laughed. "He got tangled up in the framework of that flying saucer the kids built!"

"I don't think anything's funny," Karen said. She went out on the porch to check on Joey, and Mack finished his beer and set the bottle carefully in the line he had made with the others.

"Well?" I demanded. "Am I right?"

"As far as you go."

"What do you mean, as far as I go? What else is there?"

"You're forgetting Paula Gale's money."

"What about it?"

"If Ben Gale could be shown to have murdered his wife, he wouldn't get the money she left him."

I thought about that a minute. "Who would?"

"Her other legatee. Anne Streich."

"Anne!" *The one who finds the body*, I thought. "You're saying Anne killed her sister?"

Mack gave me a pained look. "You're putting words in my mouth, J. J. Do yourself a favor and listen."

The Sheetrock man came out of the bedroom carrying his stilts. "I'll be back tomorrow to give it the last coat," he said.

"Okay."

The guy gave Mack's assembled bottles an astonished look and tramped on outdoors through the kitchen. He said something to Karen on his way past the porch. She came back in.

"Well, what, then?" I asked Mack.

"Anne's married, dummo. Her husband manages her money. Got it now?"

I shook my head. Mack shook his sadly.

"Harry Streich put Gale up to the whole thing, as soon as Anne told him her sister wanted a divorce. All he did was give Eileen—okay, Linda—the book with the passage underlined. She's a bright kid. She got the idea right away."

"Harry put him up to it," I repeated.

"He knows his brother-in-law very well. Gale's ruthless—he has a very high opinion of his own plans—but he always gets a little careless. Like forgetting Amant's wallet."

"What about David?" Karen asked. "Harry wouldn't endanger his own son!"

"That had nothing to do with Harry," Mack said. "That was pure Benjamin Gale. Harry just figured Gale would murder Paula, nice and clean and simple, and then Harry would go find all his little careless mistakes, evidence that would convict him. But Harry didn't figure on Amant's coming to the house, either, and he didn't know just when Gale would go through with it. By the time he heard Paula was dead, Amant already had the evidence, including the book with the passage underlined and 'Lala?' in Harry Streich's handwriting in the margin."

I thought of Anne's stricken look as she picked up the Xerox the night before, of my own later feeling that something was wrong.

"What happened to the book?" Karen asked.

"Probably still in Illinois," Mack said. "We're working on that."

Along with the negatives of the pictures, I thought. And the plastic bag was probably a substitute too. Gale couldn't have looked into the envelope before he shot Amant. Careless.

"So Harry couldn't do anything," Mack continued. "At first he thought Gale had just been smarter than he'd given him credit for and had ditched all the evidence. Then he tried his own blackmail approach, to see what reaction he got. And he didn't get a rise. Gale was stonewalling, but Streich didn't know that. So he backed off to think things over. He couldn't be *sure* Gale had murdered his wife, remember. There'd been an autopsy."

"Now I know what people mean when they talk about their heads swimming," Karen remarked.

"Meanwhile, Gale felt like he couldn't handle both of them, and cooked up the plan to get rid of Amant."

"Some recipe," Karen said.

"Too complicated." Mack belched. "Bound to trip him up sooner or later. We may take our time, but we get these things checked out. But like I said, that had nothing to do with Harry—he didn't even know Amant was Paula's boyfriend until last night."

"His own nephew," Karen said, of Ben.

"Makes you wonder, don't it?" Mack shook his head and burped again. "Then, after the fire, when he couldn't find the envelope in your house, Gale got another bright idea. He went to Harry all on his high horse and said what was this business of killing his wife? Accused Harry of it, said J. J. had shown him a Xerox of the book, with the passage underlined and Harry's handwriting on it."

"Oboy," I said, shaking my own head.

"Harry asked Gale to help him get it back, and Gale 'let' himself be talked into it. Neither of them knew you'd handed it over to us. Gale didn't tell Harry about trying to burn down your house, or he'd have had to explain about Linda–Eileen. As far as Harry knew, she was alive and well."

Mack held out his empty. I shook my head.

"You're probably right," he admitted, and set the bottle down beside the others. "Gale suggested they could scare you into handing it over. So old Harry, who if you didn't know has quite a reputation as a practical joker, thought of a real good scare, one that just might solve all their problems. He wasn't about to kill anybody with his own hands, and he wasn't sure what he could ask of Ben. So he came up with the tiger idea, because of CATCH."

"CATCH!" What would Prunella think?

"Any nut who chases flying saucers might just climb into a cage with a tiger, Harry figured."

Karen and I proved our marital empathy by rolling our eyes in unison.

[175]

"You didn't think one turkey did that, did you?" Mack asked. "By himself, nobody to cover his back? Gale met Harry outside the house when he came home that night and told him you were inside with Anne. They winged it from there."

"Didn't Anne know?" Karen asked.

"Separate bedrooms." Mack leered briefly. "Aren't you glad you're poor? Harry left her a note while she was taking J. J. over to the motel, saying he was tired, do not disturb, et cetera, et cetera. So far as she knew, he was asleep. Meanwhile, he had delayed you long enough for Gale to get over to the motel ahead of you. Gale knocked you out, loaded you into the Rabbit, and came by and picked up Harry. Said he had borrowed the Rabbit because his own car was in the shop." Mack cocked an eyebrow at me. "I bet it was a real temptation to hit you a little too hard."

I put my head in my hands and groaned.

"Would have given the whole game away, though," Mack reflected. "Gale was at least smart enough to see that. Enterprising types, both of them. You know what Streich said? He just couldn't stand to see Gale put all that money in thirty-month certificates."

He stood up and rubbed his belly and yawned. "Well, I got to be going if I expect to get any sleep today. Thanks for the beer. Still want me to call you if I get any UFO reports?"

"Sure," I said, standing myself. "Why not?"

"Oh, Joe!" Karen said, and sat down again fast.